The Hometown Hero
Includes Bonus Novella
Justice
Paperback Copyright © 2021 Lorhainne Ekelund
Editor: Talia Leduc

Give feedback on the book at:
lorhainneeckhart@hotmail.com

Twitter: @LEckhart
Facebook: AuthorLorhainneEckhart

Printed in the U.S.A

THE HOMETOWN HERO

The O'Connells

LORHAINNE ECKHART

The O'Connells of Livingston, Montana, are not your typical family. Follow them on their journey to the dark and dangerous side of love in a series of romantic thrillers you won't want to miss. Raised by a single mother after their father's mysterious disappearance eighteen years ago, the six grown siblings live in a small town with all kinds of hidden secrets, lies, and deception. Much like the contemporary family romance series focusing on the Friessens, this romantic suspense series follows the lives of the O'Connell family as each of the siblings searches for love.

The O'Connells

The Neighbor
The Third Call
The Secret Husband
The Quiet Day
The Commitment, An O'Connell Novella
The Missing Father
The Hometown Hero

Justice
The Family Secret
The Fallen O'Connell
The Return of the O'Connells
And The She Was Gone
The Stalker
The O'Connell Family Christmas
The Girl Next Door
Broken Promises
The Gatekeeper

The O'Connells Box Set Collections

The O'Connells Books 1 - 3
The O'Connells Books 4 - 6
The O'Connells Books 7 - 9
The O'Connells Books 10 - 12

"No matter how much you think you want to know about something, sometimes the truth is worse."

Catlou

"This book left me an emotional mess. It provoked so many raw emotions that I found myself looking for tissues more than once while reading.

Rebmay

"Another powerful story from Ms. Eckhart! Lots of mystery and intrigue!"

Kathy, Goodreads Reviewer

In this shocking O'Connell family novel, a brother's secret is exposed, opening up old wounds and creating a scandal that could rock the community.

Big brother Owen O'Connell was only sixteen when his father mysteriously disappeared, forcing him to become a father figure to his five younger siblings. If you were to ask them, they'd say Owen is the perfect older brother with the perfect life: He's single, a plumber, working his own hours in a close-knit community. Owen, though, knows that appearances are often deceiving.

When he is called to a plumbing emergency at the local high school after a grad prank goes wrong, he finds his old rival Tessa Brooks, now a teacher, holding a broken pipe in the middle of the flood, thinking she can fix the problem. However, the two soon make a horrifying discovery: the body of a student tucked away in a closet.

The event brings authorities flocking in, and in the ensuing chaos, Owen realizes that someone knows too much about his family. Having carefully held the family together since his father disappeared, he is determined to keep their secrets right where they are, dead and buried. But sometimes, secrets get revealed in the most scandalous of ways.

Chapter One

Owen O'Connell, eldest of six, couldn't remember what it was like not to have responsibility resting upon his now broad shoulders. He couldn't remember a time when he didn't have an eye on his younger siblings, worried about something they'd done or could do, or something that could come after any one of them. Even though everyone was grown now, with their own lives, he still felt that kind of responsibility. Though it hadn't been his choice, he couldn't shake the incessant need to know what was going on with his three brothers and two sisters, considering they all found their way into their own brands of trouble. The biggest lesson of all, which he'd learned long ago, was not to share anything with anyone about his life or his family's.

He took in his home workshop, a small garage at the back of his two-bedroom bungalow at the edge of town. The cottage to his right was owned by an old woman in her nineties, now in a nursing home, whose grandson had been considerate enough to move in and share his love of hip-hop with the entire neighborhood every night after midnight.

The place on the left was a rundown rental with three feet of perpetually overgrown grass, but at least they were quiet.

In the back of his van, were the box of elbow PVC pipes he'd just bought to replenish his supply. The van was faded, older. It was missing his company name, O'Connell's Plumbing, but considering he didn't need to drum up business, as most everyone knew who he was, a company decal would've been wasted dollars. If anything, Owen was the one O'Connell who couldn't and wouldn't part with one dime unnecessarily.

He spotted the ancient rusty Datsun as it pulled up and parked behind his van. The engine purred before it shut off, and the squeal of the car door revealed Lori Kramer, slender and five foot five, with sandy blond hair that stopped at her shoulders. Her pretty face still bore the pissed-off expression that had been there since their fight outside the diner where she worked as a waitress. Their on again, off again relationship, which was non-committal and, as far as he was concerned, had no strings attached, no longer worked for her. So what had she done but demand he figure his shit out, as if he were the one who had issues? He didn't, he told himself, but those had pretty much been her exact words: his issues, his lack of commitment.

Finally, because he could feel her drawing closer and hear her flip-flops on the pavement, he was forced to lift his gaze, taking in the godawful mustard dress uniform from the diner and the small box she was carrying. He put down an old pipe, wiped his hands on a damp cloth, and gave her everything, seeing the spark in her brown eyes, the light freckles over the bridge of her nose. She dumped the small box on the workbench beside him, and he took in some things of his: a shirt, a toothbrush, some old tools he'd used while fixing her sink, and a watch he hadn't missed. He wasn't sure what else was in there. When he lifted his gaze to her, she didn't say anything for another second.

"Your things." She gestured rather forcefully.

He lifted the old shirt, which he'd forgotten about, and said nothing, taking in everything in the box. He wasn't too inclined to respond.

"You know, I asked you to pick up your things," she said. "Since I didn't hear from you, here I am, driving them out to you. This is just one more reason we're not together, Owen. I can't get you to actually be part of a relationship, to show up, to follow through on anything. You want me only when you want me..."

He let out a rough sigh, knowing she was about to go on and on to fill the silence, something she always did. There was a point he stopped listening and a point at which he was just done, like now.

"I get it," he said. "Apologies. Sorry you had to make the trip over. Anything else?" He rested his hand on the box and took in her face, her lips, which he'd kissed so many times. He liked her, but even now, this situation seemed to be heading fast to confrontation, all because of her need to argue, to push, to get him to...what? Be serious about her when his focus was everywhere else.

As she'd so explicitly put it, she wanted the kind of commitment he could never see in their relationship.

"That's it? That's all I get?' She gestured between them quite dramatically. What the hell did she want from him?

He laughed. "Jesus Christ, Lori, what the fuck is this? We're over. You've said your piece already—repeatedly. I get it. You don't need to hammer it to death, if that's what this is. This isn't working. Sometimes things don't. That's life. Again, thanks for bringing my stuff, but I've got nothing else for you. Not sure what you want me to say."

He knew he sounded like an asshole, but he just rested his forearm on the box and flicked his hand. This was something else she did, push and push when things didn't quite go the way she wanted. He could see she just didn't want to let it go, and her anger seemed to hold her where she was.

"Look, I'm sorry," he said. "Is that what you want to hear from me? I can't feel something just because you want me to. It doesn't work that way. You've made your feelings clear, as I've made mine. I'm not in the same space you are, because of..."

"Yes, because of your family, I know," she snapped. "You're all about the O'Connells. Your nose is in all of their lives. All I wanted was to be included. You spend almost every night with them, but I thought maybe I would get tossed a crumb of what's left of you. You never took me once to meet your family. We weren't there yet. You never came out and said those exact words, but getting you to talk and express any kind of reasonable emotion is beyond me. I started to realize we were never going to get 'there,'" she said, complete with air quotes.

He sighed. "Okay, this has been fun, but I've got work to do, and I'm not rehashing this same old conversation about how you don't understand me. I don't understand you, either, or your need to share everything..." His phone rang, and for a second, he thought the gods were smiling down on him with the interruption. He reached for it, taking in the fact that Lori was still standing there. "I have to take this," he said.

She inclined her head, but she didn't move. Great, so she wanted to take another chunk out of his ass.

He answered and pressed his phone to his ear, giving Lori his back as he took in the rest of his shop. "Yeah? Owen here."

"Owen, this is Rita Mae, down at the high school. We've got ourselves kind of a problem down here, a plumbing emergency. There's water everywhere. It's coming from the second-floor girls' bathroom. We're not sure what happened, but..."

"Okay, on my way. Has anyone shut the main water valve off yet?" He turned around and took in Lori still standing there, her arms crossed, taking in everything he was saying.

"No, custodial is gone for the day. I have a call in to them."

Owen shook his head. "No, look, I'm on my way. I'll be there in less than ten."

He'd shut the main off himself, find out what the problem was, and fix it. At least this was his get-away-from-Lori card, he thought as he hung up and pocketed his phone. He could sense that she just didn't want to let go of this fight. He reached for his keys, giving his shop one last look, but everything he'd need—all the tools and supplies—was already in his van for exactly this reason.

"I have to go, Lori, an emergency call," he said and started walking out of his shop. When she didn't move for a second, he reached up to pull the garage door down, waiting until she finally did. She had realized this was it, and she walked past him and out of the shop.

He pulled down the door and slipped on the lock that would keep out no one who really wanted to get in. Her Datsun was still parked behind his van, and she stopped at her door and took him in. For a minute, he thought she was going to start in on him again. That was just something she did—another reason, he realized, why not seeing her had actually lifted a weight off him. Lori, although fun at times, could be a lot to handle.

"Lori, I'm sorry," he said. "I don't know how many ways I can say it, but it's over. I'm not where you are. I hope you find someone who can give you what you're looking for, but it's not me. You said it, and you were right, so let's just leave it at that."

She opened her mouth as if to say something, but she let out a sigh instead. Evidently, she'd changed her mind. She shook her head, slipped into her vehicle, started the old heap, and pulled away.

And instead of feeling sad at the ending of their relationship, he felt relieved.

Chapter Two

Owen took in the local high school and the few teens in the parking lot, because school was now out for the day. He remembered the concrete institution fondly, but he thought that was mostly nostalgia, because it was also a reminder that for him and his siblings, school hadn't been a happy social time. Today, if you asked him, he wouldn't be able to recall any of the fundamental knowledge that had been crammed into them back then.

He pulled his tool kit from the van, looping the strap over his shoulder. In just his faded blue T-shirt, he felt the chill in the air as he pulled out his phone and saw Karen's text: *Can you pick up some wine on your way over? Jack and I have to meet with a client and are running late.*

Right, everyone was going to Marcus and Charlotte's new house, which they'd just signed the papers on, across from Ryan and Jenny's. At least Marcus was now married, with a baby on the way, and then there was his adoption of Eva. Marcus, out of all of them, was the one who had really pulled his shit together.

Owen strode up the sidewalk, seeing the cracks in the

cement and remembering the spot where he'd dropped his history teacher's keys into the freshly poured concrete. Helga Adams had made every day in that class a living hell for him. To this day, he'd never shared with anyone the fact that he was the one who had taken her keys from her desk. Even though she'd accused him, she'd never been able to prove it.

He pulled open the front door and spotted Rita Mae, redheaded and slender, about ten years his senior, coming from the office. Evidently, she'd been waiting for him, as she hurried his way. His sneakers squeaked on the industrial concrete floor, looking right and left to see if anything out there was coming his way—just a habit he couldn't shake.

"Owen, thank goodness you're here," Rita Mae said. "It's quite a mess. There's water everywhere, and I don't know what to make of what happened. You know, every year about this time, I expect those seniors to pull something. When I heard there was water coming down the stairs from the girls' bathroom, I just knew it was them. I hope it's not going to be too bad! It seems the kids are getting more creative every year with their so-called pranks, which are destructive to school property. From the toilet paper decorating the entire hall to Mr. Goodman's motorcycle on the roof of the school last year—though how they got it up there, I have no idea—and now this, something just has to be done with those kids…"

He was following Rita Mae down the hall, and he took in how quiet the place was. "So, speaking of misfits, where're all the kids?" he added as he started up the stairs. "Seems rather quiet, considering."

"You're right," she said. "School's out for the day, and we don't see many sticking around, maybe a few here and there. It's amazing, though. Today it's absolutely deserted, which tells me every kid in the school likely knew this was going to happen and skedaddled instead of having to answer questions and face the music. What is it with teenagers?"

He wondered whether she expected him to answer. He took in the water on the stairs, a thin stream. As his feet splashed through the puddles, he realized Rita Mae was still talking, carrying on about the seniors. He knew well those kinds of pranks, that kind of trouble. The O'Connells had been neck deep in it at one time.

Marcus had been the worst. Any time trouble happened at school, nine times out of ten, Marcus had been behind it, had known about it, or had been a part of it. Then there was Ryan. Owen had lost count of the number of times he'd pulled his younger brothers out of something: doing graffiti, keying the principal's car, letting air out of the science teacher's tires... His other younger brother, Luke, had pretty much taken care of himself. Karen was one he'd had to watch extra closely, and then there was Suzanne, who had always given the impression that everything was fine even when it wasn't. Now look at them. He wondered if he'd ever be able to shake his need to herd them all, to keep tabs on all of them.

As he topped the stairs, he spotted the sheen of water coming from the bathroom just ahead, where the door was open. He found himself looking at the concrete block walls, the girls' sign on the open door.

Rita Mae went in first and peered around the corner. "Owen is here now. OMG, look at you, girl! This mess..."

He wasn't sure whom she was talking to at first, but as he stepped into the bathroom, he saw her: her blond hair pulled back into a neat bun, her slender curves in navy slacks and a white tank top, her flat shoes in the water on the floor. The paneling had been pulled off the wall that led to the plumbing, and he could see the wrench in her hand. She was reaching as high as she could on tiptoes to bang the red valve, which he knew was the water shut-off.

She turned her head. All the while, water was still spraying out from what he could now see was a busted pipe. For a second, he felt shocked, looking into her face, oval perfection. Her white tank left nothing to the imagination, soaked. She could've won a wet T-shirt contest, as it was practically sheer over her perfect breasts. He had to remind himself this was Tessa Brooks, his first crush, though that had crashed and burned, and she was now just an old rival.

Right. Someone had mentioned long ago that she was now a teacher.

"Well, are you going to do something, or are you going to just stand there and keep staring at my breasts?" she said, then made a rude noise. He thought she'd dropped the F-bomb under her breath. Right, she also had a smart mouth. He'd forgotten about that.

She turned back around and gripped the wrench, about to swing it and pound away at the red lever again, so he reached out and grabbed her wrist, holding it just as she went to swing again. It was that damn competitive drive, as if she thought she could do everything better than him.

"Whoa, what the hell, Tessa? Stop before you break something." He went to take the wrench, but she seemed to grip it harder, giving him everything in that one look. He was still holding her wrist, but he didn't let go, just stepped in right beside her. She was tall and slender, with perfect curves, about five inches shorter than him. *Pull it together, Owen.* Her eyes were blue, vivid, and flashing with hellfire —and then there were those lips.

"Take your hands off me," she said, enunciating each

word carefully through gritted teeth so there was no chance he'd misunderstand.

Water was still spraying out, soaking his shirt now too, and what did he do but put his other hand on the wrench to pry it from her? He tossed it onto the floor in the water, then somehow maneuvered her back and reached up to shut off the water. The spray stopped, and the water slowly drizzled and then dripped.

"It was one hand, Tessa," he said. "Now that I'm here, you can let a professional fix this before you break something and turn what'll likely be a simple fix into something far more costly and time-consuming."

She didn't pull those magnificent blue eyes from him. She could tell him to fuck off with just a look, and he could see she was likely thinking of a way to tell him how she could and would do things better than he would.

"I was trying to turn the water off and almost had it, Owen."

He knew she hated him. At the same time, everything about her brought up unsettling and frustrating feelings inside him. He took in the counter, seeing the gray duct tape, and he reached for it and lifted it. Rita Mae had evidently realized she was in the middle of something personal and had quietly stepped out.

"You planning on doing something with this?" Owen said, tossing the duct tape back on the wet counter and setting his tool case beside one of the sinks. He took a better look at the busted pipe, wondering what had caused this. He doubted this was a prank. More than likely, from the looks of it, the pipe was just old and had been about to give for some time.

"I was planning on fixing the pipe," she snapped. "I was going to turn the water off and then duct tape it until it could be fixed. You know, I'm not completely useless, Owen. I have two hands and the ability to problem-solve, which was exactly what I was doing. Then here you are, showing up and thinking I'm out of my depth. I'll have you know I had a handle on the situation, and—"

"Are you finished?" He cut her off, facing her.

She was standing there, holding her ground. The woman was infuriating, and he quickly remembered how she never had gone quietly into the night. No, scratch that. She had never sat back and counted on him for anything. As if she had realized how indecent her shirt was, she simply crossed her arms under those amazing breasts and gave him everything.

Confidence. Two can play this game.

"Evidently," she said, then gestured to the tools and the sink. "I'll leave you to this, then."

He had expected something else from her. No, he had *wanted* something else. Her walking away that easily should've been a relief, but there was something about her attitude that he craved. What was it about Tessa? He had anticipated fighting with her, sparring with her, because their arguments had been on another level. No other woman could compete.

"So how did this happen?" he added, taking in her confusion as she stepped back. "Rita Mae said it was a school prank, seniors, but these pipes are old, no longer up to code. Corrosion and wear is what this looks like."

He took in the pipes intently only because he was finding it damn difficult to keep his gaze from her. When he reached up for the red shut-off lever, he felt how corroded that was, as well.

"I have no idea," she said. "I was in my classroom, finishing up for the day, and was just about ready to pack it up and leave when something caught my eye. I stepped out of my classroom to investigate and saw water everywhere. I followed it into the bathroom here and found all this..."

As she gestured, someone screamed. In the second that followed, Tessa gave him everything before darting out the door ahead of him. Around the corner, he spotted Rita Mae standing outside a room labeled *Janitor*, staring down at something in shock.

As he stepped behind both women and took in the closet, he realized what the problem was. He was staring at the body of a young man, curled up, unmoving. On pure instinct, he moved both Rita Mae and Tessa aside and crouched down, seeing the lifeless eyes of what looked like a student. He reached in and checked for a pulse, but just looking at him, he already knew he was dead.

Chapter Three

"Look, I have no idea what the hell happened," Owen said to Marcus, his brother, the sheriff, as he took in the scene at the school. "I was called to a plumbing emergency. There was water everywhere."

He'd pulled out his phone and called Marcus after making the discovery, which had brought in what seemed like everyone. Tessa was talking with one of the crime scene techs, and Harold, his brother's lead deputy and Suzanne's partner, was speaking with Rita Mae. He took in the body, which had been photographed and was now in a body bag, being wheeled away. Another deputy, Lonnie, was in the bathroom, and the kid deputy, Colby, was directing the emergency workers to move the body down the stairs.

Owen was still having a hard time shaking the fact that he'd found a kid in a closet, dead. It was surreal, the entire scene.

"Any idea who the kid is?" Owen said. His arms were crossed, and he glanced around, taking in everyone. Tessa ran her hand over the back of her neck, strong and confident but shaken as all hell. He could see it only because he knew her better than he was comfortable with. Tessa had a diffi-cult independent personality, and anyone else would've had to look real hard to see it.

"Jackson Moore," Marcus said. "You know the Moore family? He's one of Susan's four kids. A hard call that'll be."

Owen winced. The Moores had been in Livingston as long as his family had—longer, maybe. He could see this was the part of the job his brother didn't like. Who would want to face parents and tell them their kid was dead? This was the kind of thing that just didn't happen in their town.

"You said the water's off?" Marcus said. "We're going to have to shut this down for now, so you won't be fixing anything for a bit. We need to investigate, find out what happened. With all the kids and everyone in the school, it's going to be like finding a needle in a haystack—or we could get lucky."

From the way his brother said it, he knew that was wishful thinking. But then, someone had to have seen something.

"Fine, I get it," Owen said. "School will be out too, then. I'll fix it when you give the all clear. How old was Jackson, anyway?" He didn't know why he needed to ask. It was irrelevant now, but he just wanted to know.

"Pretty sure he's Alison's age," Marcus said. "What a waste. He never even had a chance at life, at screwing up or choosing something or creating something... Shit!"

The door was still open, and Owen took in the small closet, how dark it would've been, still filled with cleaning supplies, brooms, mops, and janitorial equipment. He didn't know what to think.

"So was he murdered?" Owen said. He knew he'd never get the sightless eyes of the young man out of his mind. It was never supposed to happen this way—a wasted life. What the hell had happened?

The look from Marcus was one he knew well. "You know I can't talk about that. It's too early, anyway. Coroner will need to figure it out. Couldn't see anything, any visible marks to give us a clue. How the hell did he get into that closet? Why was he there?"

There was a lot to figure out. He looked around, seeing how upset Rita Mae was. Harold was walking over toward them, calm, collected, together, one of his brother's best deputies. Marcus reached out and touched his shoulder. "I'll have someone grab your tools, but this is a crime scene now. Let me know if you hear of something. Keep your ear to the ground, and let me know if you think of anything that could help."

He watched as his brother moved away with Harold, discussing crime-scene things that he knew had nothing to do with him. He took in Tessa, for the first time realizing she was completely out of sorts. It took her another second before she realized he was walking right toward her. He could hear Rita Mae crying, but he kept walking.

"You okay?" was all he said as he stopped in front of Tessa, whose shirt was still damp and indecent. He gestured helplessly. He didn't even have a jacket to give her.

"Sure. Seriously? Of course I'm not. That was Jackson Moore. He was one of my students. How is it possible that he's dead? It's wrong, so wrong that this could happen. What the hell was he doing in that closet, anyways?" She lifted her hands and then let them fall helplessly to her sides. "Any idea what happened, how he died?"

The more he looked, the more he saw something in her blue eyes that made him not want to walk away. She didn't show this side of herself to just anyone. There was just something about her. He sensed her vulnerability.

He shook his head. He knew she was asking the same questions he was. "Where're your things?" he said. "We should grab them and then go."

She lifted her hand in a gesture and started to one of the classrooms down the hall. Inside, he took in the empty desks, the old chalkboard, the same as when he'd gone to school. She opened a drawer and pulled out her purse, then tucked a laptop from the desk into a case. He took in the cream-colored sweater looped around the back of the chair and reached for it.

"Here, put this on," he said, holding it up, taking in those blue eyes that seemed to connect with him for just a second. Would she argue? "Tessa, your shirt. Come on, you have to be cold. You're still wet."

She must've known, as she slipped her arms into her sweater, and he rested his hands over her shoulders, feeling her tension and the stress of the moment. He let his hands linger. Of course she was upset. He could feel it.

There was something about her hair, that fine blond hair. He ran his fingers over the strands that fell here and there from her bun, then tucked a few strands behind her ear and let his hand fall away. He made himself step back.

She didn't pull her questioning gaze. For a moment, he was positive she was fighting the urge to lean closer. He could see it. At the same time, she wouldn't let herself. He gestured to the door behind him and then ran his hand over her shoulder again and around her back to steer her there.

"We should go," he said. "I'll walk you out."

She was about to shake her head. He could just tell when a woman wanted something even though she denied it, but Tessa was a master of control, of making sure she would never have the one thing she wanted. She didn't give in, and he was well aware he was as stubborn as she was.

"You don't have to," she said. "I'm a big girl, Owen. I can look after myself. Been doing it for years."

At any other time, he'd have said fine and walked away, but something about the situation had him digging his heels in. "No," he said. "I'm sure you're capable of looking after yourself, Tessa, but seriously, a kid just died. Don't be so damn stubborn. You're upset, I'm upset. Be human for a second. This isn't about that. Let's go. I'll walk you out."

He could sense without her saying a word that she was happy he was insisting. Her hand was on her computer bag, and he reached for it and took it from her. He didn't know how he did it, but he had her walking out of the room. He took in the cops, the crime scene, and Marcus, who was talking to one of them but gave Owen a look. Something passed between them as he led Tessa out to the stairs, where water was still running down in a thin stream.

"Careful on the stairs," he said. "It'll be slippery." He just couldn't help himself. He let her go first as she held the rail.

"You know, Owen, you don't have to walk me out. I already told you..."

"You've said that already, Tessa. Just stop it, okay? This isn't the time to be so stubborn."

She stepped down off the last step and looked up to him, and for a moment, he could see she might be having trouble with something.

"Any idea of what happened?" she said. "I mean, Jackson was kind of a loner. He had a few friends in class, but he kept his head down. Why would he have been in that closet?" She lifted her hands, adjusting her purse over her shoulder. She was struggling and wasn't about to leave it alone. Could he blame her? Hell, he needed a shot of something after this.

He somehow maneuvered her around and had her walking to the front door again. The questions kept circling in his mind, too. "Rita Mae said something about a prank, about how she was waiting for something. Know anything about that?"

"You mean the grad pranks from the seniors that happen every year around this time?" She was so close to him as she walked, and he opened the front door and gestured for Tessa to go first. She did, but she seemed to linger a bit as if waiting for him, then fell in beside him again, walking down the steps.

He took in the flashing lights of the emergency vehicles. She gestured to a light blue compact in the parking lot not far from his plumbing van.

"Yeah, those ones," he said.

She sighed as she kept walking, and he pressed his hand to her lower back because he just couldn't keep from touching her. "Honestly, I don't know, Owen. With the deserted halls and the flooding, that was honestly my first thought, too. It seems as if someone knew something..."

She stopped at her car and let out a sigh, then reached into her purse and pulled out her keys. He watched the way she clutched them, then hesitated, looking over the roof of her car as if thinking some heavy thoughts.

"You good to drive? I can follow you home," he added.

She gave him everything again. "What happened between us, Owen?"

There it was, the million-dollar question. He was too stubborn, and so was she. "Life, everything...nothing," he said, then shrugged, knowing it wasn't an answer. He didn't know when it was that his feelings for her had changed, which single moment had had him walking away. She didn't pull her gaze from him, and Owen didn't step back.

He found himself nodding. "You want to grab a drink?"

She said nothing for a second, giving him everything. Her eyes, the blueness... No one could compete with her. He expected a no, hell no, but instead she clutched her keys and seemed to consider it. "Yeah, a drink seems appropriate. So where?"

"Pop your things in your car, and I'll drive. The Lighthouse?"

She held her keys up, and he saw that part of her that never went quietly as she said, "The Lighthouse sounds great, but I'll drive."

Chapter Four

"Never realized you were a gin and tonic woman," Owen said, taking in Tessa as she sat on the bar stool beside him, leaning on the old dark wood bar top and swirling a plastic stir stick in her drink after squeezing in a lime.

"And I never expected you to just get in my car and let me drive," she replied. She tapped the stick on the edge of her glass and set it on the bar counter, then lifted the glass and took a swallow.

Owen gripped his double shot of whiskey. A pint of beer wasn't going to do it for him. He needed something stronger and with a bite.

"There you go, not answering," she said. "Why do you do that? I don't get it. This here..." She gestured between them.

He stood and leaned beside her, not missing the scent of lavender. Maybe it was her shampoo or soap, but it was one of the little things about her that unsettled him. "What don't you get?" he said, though he knew damn well what she was getting at, and he didn't need to be such a prick about it.

He sensed the minute she was about to get up and leave, so he reached out and grabbed her arm before she could slip off the stool. "Sorry," he said. "Look, I don't know why I do that." He did, but saying that was easier than answering, because sharing anything with anyone was something he never did.

She gave him everything, standing so close now that he could feel her.

He could have stepped back, but he didn't want to. "Sit down and finish your drink," he said. Any other woman would have sat down and finished, but there was something about Tessa that wasn't easy or uncomplicated. He sighed. "Please, Tessa, come on."

"You going to keep avoiding answering me and playing games? Because I have to say, Owen, it's the quality I like the least about you." It was so matter of fact, the way she said it, that for a minute he really took her in, and he didn't miss the sincerity mixed in with all the annoyance.

"Sorry, it's not deliberate. Just a habit, I guess." He swirled his whiskey and took a swallow, looking around, seeing faces he knew. When he gave her everything again, he saw the confusion on her face, as if she were thinking. What he'd have given to know what was going on in that head of hers.

"It's a damn annoying habit, Owen."

He leaned on the bar beside her as she sat back on her stool, lifted her glass, and took a swallow of her drink.

"What do you want to know?" he said.

"As in, ask you anything?"

What was it about that question that had him wanting to roll his shoulders and shake off the feeling that was setting him on edge?

"Geez, you can't even hide how uncomfortable you are

at that simple question, as if there's something you don't want anyone to know."

"No, seriously, ask me." He knew it had come out rather sharply.

That brought a smile to the edges of her lips. "Fine. You never answered me about my car. I insisted on driving, and you didn't argue. I half expected you to do that thing you do and walk away or say no, or take my keys, maybe."

He couldn't help the laugh that burst out. "Take your keys? That would be something, Tessa. You'd likely have decked me."

She raised her brows. "There you go, not really answering. It's as if you have this secret that you need to hide. Now I'm convinced there's really something there. Do you have a secret, Owen?"

The way she asked had him finishing his whiskey and lifting his hand to the bartender. "No secret," he said. "And, honestly, I don't know why I just let you drive. With the shitshow we walked out of at the school, the bad scene, it didn't feel right to argue. Evidently, you didn't want to give up control by getting into my van and driving with me, so I let you have this one. So what about you, Tessa? Why are you so driven? Why the need to do it yourself? Everything about you, it seems, is a fight. If I say blue, I'm pretty sure you'd say red."

The bartender strode over.

"You want another drink?" Owen said.

Tessa just shook her head. "I'm good."

"I'll take a pint of your ale," Owen said. "Bring another gin and tonic, too," he added, taking in the shock on Tessa's face when the bartender walked away.

"I said no. What don't you understand about that?"

He wanted to laugh at her, at the fire and fight. Anyone

else would've likely taken the damn drink. "Force of habit, I guess—and I'm not drinking alone."

Her lips twitched, and she inclined her head. "Okay, you'll get a pass for today only, but I'm not getting drunk, so if that's your plan..."

What was it about her? He could go back and forth with her all day. "No, not my plan, but if I recall, just a second ago, you were busting my balls about evading and not answering, yet here you are, doing the same thing."

She stilled as she lifted her glass, and for a second, as she gave him everything, he could see how she hadn't expected that.

"You've always been driven," he said. "You've never been the kind of woman to sit back and be meek and go with things. I always expect a fight about everything with you, as if you can see only your way and think only you can do it. Why?" He wondered if she'd answer.

She lowered her gaze and then flicked those blue eyes up to him. "Okay. What if I say I don't know, and it's just who I am?"

He was shaking his head. "Bullshit," he said just as a pint of ale appeared in front of him, along with a short glass of gin and tonic with a twist of lime on the side for Tessa.

"Thank you," she said with a smile and a lift of her chin to the bartender. It faded as she gripped her glass and lifted it, finishing off her first drink and then sliding the glass away to reach for the second one. "I don't want to be disappointed," she said. "I just find it easier, and it hurts less to be the one deciding for myself. The moment I depend on anyone, I'm disappointed and hurt. I don't like feeling that way, and yes, it's about not being in control of things that affect me. I learned long ago to do things by myself, so if that's what you're seeing..." She gestured at herself. He could see how uncomfortable she was.

"So who hurt you? Who is it that disappointed you, Tessa?" he said, though he didn't think she'd answer. For all the years he'd known her, there was still so much about her that he didn't know.

"I don't know," she said. "I guess it was just my dad, all the times he said he'd do something and then wouldn't, all the broken promises. To him, they were little things. Something always came up, from the trip he talked about, to the bike he promised me, or a game, an event, a show, dinner. There was always something, as far back as I can remember. I'd get excited about something and then wait all week for that one thing, and then he'd have a bad day at work, or something would happen, and my parents would say that was life and I needed to get over it. I learned the promises he made were just dreams that would never happen, so after that, with anything anyone said, I knew if I counted on someone, I'd be disappointed. So yeah, I did it myself, everything." She was self-assured and unapologetic.

He took her in, considering the thing he'd never known about her. "So you automatically think everyone is out to disappoint you and can't be trusted to follow through on something? You think you're the only one who can do it right? Correct me if I'm wrong, but that's what it sounds like to me."

She furrowed her brow, and for a moment, he thought she'd argue. "You make me sound horrible, Owen." She lifted her chin to him, and he could see how she'd gone from semi-relaxed to overthinking.

"No, I don't think you're horrible by any means, Tessa. I never said that, so don't put words in my mouth. I'm sorry your dad did that, but don't you think by assuming everyone will let you down, that's exactly the expectation you're putting out there for everyone? Sometimes you can set standards so high, Tessa, that no one can meet them. Not everyone is your dad, but sometimes stuff does come up."

He didn't move from where he was, so close to her. He could see this topic was associated with hurts buried beneath so many layers, and getting to the bottom of it was like peeling an onion.

"I won't apologize for who I am, Owen." She gave him everything as she set her glass down. Was she considering leaving?

"I'm not sure why you think I expect an apology," he said.

It was there in her face, her expression, as she shrugged. "Well, you just said you think my standards are too high."

He made a rude noise. "Don't think that's what I said. I'm just questioning your motives, is all. That's all that is, Tessa. I'm not in your head, but most folks are just doing the best they can."

She pulled in a breath, and he didn't miss the way her chest rose. He couldn't pull his gaze from the curve of her breasts as he dragged his gaze back up to her face. She could never be lost, even in a sea of pretty women. None of the women he'd dated could hold a candle to Tessa in personality. He held her gaze and took in her gorgeous pink lips, her narrow nose, and the hairline scar on her cheekbone.

"So is that what you're doing, Owen, your best?"

He didn't know how to answer her, but he knew what she was asking. "It's who I am, Tessa. I don't know how to be any other way. May not be what you're looking for, but it is what it is." He lifted his ale and took a swallow, letting his gaze linger on her, taking in all of her.

"You have a lot of secrets, Owen."

He said nothing for another second as he took in the two of them, the bar, and the fact that he hadn't thought of the kid they'd found dead for a few minutes now.

"Don't we all, Tessa?"

This time, she lifted her drink and didn't bother to answer.

Chapter Five

His brother was waiting for him outside the school when he pulled up with Tessa. Her car was a compact stick shift, and after two drinks, it had been she who said they needed to go. He'd paid the bill, refused her money, and sat uncomfortably in the passenger side with his knees pressed to the dash.

"Pull in here and park," he said, gesturing, seeing the way Marcus and Harold both gave him everything as they talked with each other.

"You have a hard time not giving orders, don't you?" she said as she parked and pulled up the emergency brake.

"I'm a man, Tessa, and one who doesn't know how to sit back and do nothing—or is that what you would prefer?" The way he said it, he knew she understood their conversation had gone way beyond casual. Maybe it was that the two drinks had eased away the guard that seemed to be a part of who he was, who she was.

She pressed her tongue to her lip but appeared unaffected, looking straight ahead, out the windshield. Neither of them moved. He knew his brother was waiting, staring at the two of them, but at the same time, he didn't want to let Tessa off without an answer.

Her hand squeezed the knob of the gearshift, and he took in her ringless fingers. He'd never asked her about who she was seeing, and it wasn't lost on him that she hadn't, either. Every woman he met, the first thing she always asked was if he had a special someone. The answer was always no.

She gestured toward him. "Thanks for the drink, for the company, and for making this moment bearable." Then she turned her head to him, giving him everything again. He knew he had his answer from her lack of response. Even her distinct blue eyes seemed to ease and soften a bit.

He jutted his chin to his brother and then took in Tessa again. "Have dinner with me."

Her eyes widened. He knew she hadn't expected it. Hell, he couldn't believe he'd asked. She shook her head. "That's not a good idea..." she started, but he reached over and rested his hand over hers, feeling how she responded.

"It's just dinner, two old friends sharing a meal."

She shut her eyes for a second, inhaled, and he could feel her tension. His hand was still over hers. She stared down at it but made no move to pull hers free. "Why do you want to have dinner with me, Owen?"

"Does it matter why? Do I have to have a reason? Don't be difficult. Just go with it, Tessa. Don't overthink it. It's just dinner. I'll talk with Marcus, and I'll pick you up from your place." He took in her surprise.

"You mean tonight?"

He'd have laughed at her expression, considering there wasn't a woman he'd ever had to talk into dinner, into spending time with him, or into bed. "Unless you have plans," he said.

That was her out, but he didn't think she was one of

those women. He could be wrong, but Tessa had never played those kinds of games. She just didn't roll that way. "You mean other than a ton of homework to mark, lesson plans to ready for tomorrow, and Netflix to watch? No, I have no other plans."

He figured that was the only answer he was going to get. He settled his hand on the door and rested it there a second before pulling it open. "Great. I'll finish up here and see you at yours."

She nodded as he pulled his hand away and stepped out of her small car. "Owen..." she called out.

He leaned down, resting his hand on the door frame. For a second, he was positive she'd changed her mind. He said nothing but gave her everything.

"How do you know where I live?" she said.

What was he supposed to say to that? He'd always known where she was—first at the apartment she'd rented until five years ago, then at the small house she'd rented for six months by the river before moving in the middle of the night, then at the duplex she'd rented from a couple until they sold it the year before, and then the small house five blocks from his place, which she'd finally bought.

"This is a small town, Tessa. You should know that if someone isn't telling someone about someone else's business, that person doesn't live here."

And the fact was that every time her name had come up when people talked, he'd always listened.

She made a face, put her clutch in gear, and tapped the stick shift with her hand. "So who's talking about me?" she said.

This time, he allowed a mischievous smile to pull at the edge of his lips, and he winked. "I'll tell you tonight at dinner," he said, then stepped back, closed the door, and patted the roof of her car. He waited while she backed up and drove away before taking in his brother. Harold had gotten into a cruiser and was pulling out, and Marcus took a few steps toward him, all the while taking in Tessa as she drove off.

Marcus gestured with his thumb to her. "Didn't know you two were friends," he said. Owen knew Marcus likely wanted to ask a lot more than that.

"I've known Tessa a long time," Owen said. "She was upset. We went for a drink." he added.

Marcus nodded, but he seemed distracted.

"So you talked to Jackson's parents?" Owen said. The last thing he wanted to talk about with anyone was Tessa or anything about the personal side of his fucked-up life.

"Yeah," Marcus said. "I had Lonnie head over, and he broke the news. I need to speak with them later. They have a ton of questions that I don't have answers for."

He could see how this was eating up his brother. He carried a lot of weight on his shoulders, being sheriff. If he screwed up in any way, the chances of his re-election would be slim, considering all eyes were on him now.

"You have any idea how he died?"

His brother said nothing for a second. "Too early to say for sure, but the coroner said early signs show asphyxiation. From what, we don't know. Are drugs involved?" Marcus shrugged. "We'll have to wait for the tox screen to come back, and then we'll know more. We'll track down the kids from school, his friends. The school still doesn't have security cameras, but someone knows something. We'll find out. Oh, I put your tools into your van for you. I'll let you know when you can get in and do the repairs. School's closed for now, so the kids will have a few days off while we investigate."

What could he say to that?

"You think someone killed him?" Owen said. "When I showed up, Rita Mae was going on about grad pranks. You know how they go. You and Ryan were thick as thieves in everything that went down."

Marcus didn't smile, just glanced away and then winced. "Yeah, well, can't say for sure. At least I have an idea where to start, considering I was one of those kids." He patted Owen's shoulder. "You heading over to Ryan's tonight?"

He shook his head. "Not tonight. I have plans."

Marcus took him in, then looked down the road where Tessa had gone and back to him. "Tessa or someone else?"

There it was, his annoyance at anyone asking too many questions about his personal life. "Just dinner, catching up with a friend," Owen said. "See you Friday. I take it you're working late."

He thought there was a hint of a smile on Marcus's face, then another wince. "Yeah, I'm working late. I'll stop in at home, check in on Charlotte and Eva, but this is a hell of a thing. Of all the years we've lived here and all the crazy things that may have happened in this town, finding a kid dead in the janitor's closet at the school is something I never would've expected. I don't know, Owen. Whatever turns up, I just have the feeling this isn't going to have a happy ending for anyone."

Owen watched as his brother strode away to his cruiser. The emergency vehicles were still there, and there was tape across the door to mark the crime scene. As he walked to his van, he was feeling something he hadn't felt in a good many years, as if more secrets were brewing, ones that could rock his hometown.

Whatever it was, he hoped it would be resolved quickly.

He couldn't have explained that tightness in his chest, that weight he'd been carrying for so long. There were secrets he didn't talk about, which seemed to simmer in a place inside him that he'd once thought was safe from anyone.

He took in the school, pulled in a breath, and forced himself to think of Tessa. The diner where he'd once gone was exactly the place he wouldn't be taking her tonight.

Chapter Six

THERE WAS SOMETHING FAMILIAR ABOUT HER STREET, he thought as he parked in front of a faded yellow bungalow with an attached garage in front and a flower bed similar to what his mom had planted—her fall garden, as she had always called it.

He strode up the driveway behind Tessa's compact, seeing her neatly trimmed grass and the ladder leaning against the side of the house, next to gutters that needed to be put up. The door was closed, and, seeing the tape over the doorbell, he knocked instead, taking in the missing trim around the windows.

He could hear her footsteps, and then the door opened. Her wavy blond hair was now hanging long and loose, and she'd changed into a red and white blouse and faded blue jeans. For a second, she said nothing, her hand resting on the door.

He felt uncomfortable, uneasy. This sense of awkwardness was something he'd never felt from her, and he found himself taking her in, seeing a change in her, as if the moment she drove home, she'd had a chance to go back to that edginess and had realized she couldn't really like him.

How had they found themselves here?

"Why do you do that?" she said, her voice accusing.

He didn't have a clue what she was getting at. He looked past her into the house, where an empty hallway led back to a kitchen, he thought. "Do what?" he said. "Do you want me to stand out here, or are you going to invite me in?"

She gestured, and her blue eyes seemed to flash with fire for a moment as she stepped back, letting him into the house. As Owen strode inside, she closed the door, and he took in the living room off to the right with only a sectional and end tables, an old stereo, and no TV. He noted the hardwood floors, which looked almost new, and the fact that all the trim was missing.

"You always have this way about you, Owen," she said. "You stare and you say nothing. It's annoying, frankly, as if you're judging things. I never know what you're thinking, because you give nothing away when you do that. I can never tell if you love something or hate it. Why do you do that? It's really..."

He turned to her, seeing that she was still barefoot. She had stopped talking, and he realized that was likely in reaction to him. "Habit, I guess," he said. "I pick up more about people by just listening. Some people talk too much and give everything away about themselves and everyone around them. I don't think it's anyone's business what I'm thinking or feeling, so maybe that's why I do it. I notice things about people, but I never realized, I guess, how you'd take it."

And the fact was that he felt as if he'd been holding on to everyone's secrets for so long that he wasn't about to take the chance of letting anything slip by opening his mouth. It was best to say nothing. All she did was grunt. Then she strode past him and tossed a glance to him over her shoulder as he took in her place.

"You doing some renovations here?" he said, following her into an older kitchen, where it appeared she was tearing out cabinets. He spotted an electric stove and dated yellow fridge as well as power tools against one wall where a table would go.

She shrugged as she stopped at the sink and the only cupboards left in the kitchen. "I bought this at a deal, and it needed more than a few repairs. Started with a few things here and there. The floors I did myself, and I figured I could do the cupboards too, but they quickly became more than I expected, so now I have more than a few projects to keep me busy. So, dinner..."

He pulled his gaze from the wall, which had been sanded down, over to her. She was waiting for him to say something, and she had that look on her face again.

"Right, let's see. Burgers, pizza, or..."

She lifted a brow. "Or I could cook," she said. That was definitely not what he'd expected, and he wondered whether his surprise showed. "I have a salad I can whip up and some steak in the fridge," she added. It was the first time he'd sensed her uncertainty.

"Works for me," he said. "A homecooked meal. I can even barbecue, if you'd like..."

She was shaking her head, and he looked over his shoulder to the window, taking in a small overgrown back-yard. "Sorry, no barbecue," she said. "Just the stovetop, but pan fried works if you're okay with that, and I even have beer in the fridge."

He thought she was teasing him as she pulled open the fridge and held up a light canned beer, not something he drank, but he took it and cracked it open. She took one for herself and closed the fridge after taking out lettuce and one large steak and sitting them on the counter by the sink. He took a step closer to her and leaned against the fridge, lifting his beer.

"You know," she said, "I got home and realized that after finding Jackson dead, I just don't want to go out in public. Word's probably out about him and the fact that we were there, and then questions happen, you know? Considering the deputy already instructed me not to talk about what I saw..." She turned around and leaned against the sink, lifted her beer, and took a swallow.

He could see how distracted she was and how this was now taking a toll. Maybe it was the shock setting in. "I get it," he said. "I told you, dinner here is fine. You should know that school will be closed for a bit, too, until the investigation is finished, so you have a few days to get settled. I guess I never asked you how you're doing in all this. You're right: Word will get out. It always does—and rumors and stuff. You're best to just say you can't talk about it. My brother will probably also question you again to see if there's something else you remember."

The way she was looking at him, he wasn't sure what to make of it. She turned back to the sink to dump in the lettuce, then opened a cupboard and pulled out a bag of potatoes. She held up two as if wanting his approval or something.

"Sure," was all he said.

She nodded. "Any idea or word yet on how he died?"

There it was, the question he'd have given anything to answer. He just shook his head, but he didn't pull his gaze. What the hell was it about Tessa? She was the real deal—

classy, difficult, nothing easy about her, but being around her had always come too easy.

"We'll hear soon, I'm sure," he said. "The kids at the school will all be questioned to find out what they were up to, what was really going on. The police will likely track down the last kids who were there today to pin them down and question them, and they'll find out pretty quick how he got in that janitor's closet."

The location was too public, which had him thinking the death had to have been the result of some prank, maybe. Nothing thought through too well, though. That was for sure.

When his cell phone rang, Tessa watched him as he pulled it from his pocket and took in the screen, seeing his brother's name. "It's Marcus," he said as he pressed the green accept button and put the phone to his ear. "So what's up?"

"Cause of death just came back," Marcus said. "Drugs were found in his system, a type of opioid found in prescription painkillers. He had an allergic reaction and asphyxiated."

Owen couldn't help but wince. "You talk to the parents, too?"

"Yeah, and they're demanding to know where he got the drugs. It seems they were likely someone's pills. His parents said he didn't take anything, and they had nothing like that in the house. Could be a situation where some kids at school got a hold of mom or dad's prescription and passed it out, or could be something else entirely, considering his reaction. Coroner said he evidently hadn't taken them before, because of his reaction to them..."

Owen let the phone slide away from his mouth. He knew

without his brother saying so that there was likely a bunch the Moores didn't know about their son and what he had been doing. "Thanks for letting me know," he said. "I take it you're talking to the kids he hung around with, his friends?"

Tessa was still giving him everything, watching him.

"Harold's talking to a few," Marcus said. "I want to talk to Tessa again. She was his teacher, so she has an idea of which kids he hangs with. Ryan had a word with Alison."

"She knew him?"

A frown crossed Tessa's face. Of course, she could hear one side of the conversation only.

Owen hoped to all hell that Alison wasn't involved. He could feel the tension pull across his shoulders, because this would be where he shut the conversation down. Family was family.

"She knows him—sort of, she said, whatever that means, but not well. She told Ryan that Jackson was kind of a nerd, didn't really get into trouble. After some prompting when I showed up, Alison spilled that she'd heard something about some grad prank…"

"I'm almost afraid to ask," Owen cut in, pressing his finger and thumb to the bridge of his nose, feeling Tessa staring at him.

His brother wasn't laughing. He was positive he could hear something in the background, voices. Maybe he was still at Ryan's. He thought he should maybe head over and listen in on what Alison was saying.

"Yeah, well, it gets better," Marcus said. "Seems the kids were planning on running naked around the school after dropping some pills, which we're thinking were the opioids. Alison said that's all she heard. She wasn't too forthcoming on who was involved or whose bright idea it was. She said she had no plans to run naked, so she left right after school and came home, but she did give us a few names, at least. I'm about to head off, talk to those kids, and hope to all hell their parents don't shut it down."

"You sure that's all she knows?" Owen said. He knew he didn't have to say more, because Alison had been a part of their family for only a short time, and she did have a history of getting into trouble. He was sure she was on the straight and narrow right now, but he also knew that Marcus would likely tread carefully if she was involved. Maybe after he left Tessa's, he should stop by Ryan's.

"Yeah, pretty sure," Marcus said. "She was scared shit-less when she heard. Ryan said he's going to sit down with her again. Karen's over there, and Mom too. I need to talk to Tessa now. You said you're having dinner with her?"

"Yeah, I'm at her place now."

There was silence for a second on the line, and he let his gaze linger on Tessa as he took in the moment that she real-ized he was talking about her.

"Okay, so let her know I'm on my way over," Marcus said, then hung up.

Owen kept his gaze on Tessa, seeing the open question as he slid his cell phone in his back pocket. She gestured toward him.

"Marcus is on his way over," he explained. "He wants to talk to you again. Jackson took some opioids and had a reaction."

She shut her eyes, and he didn't miss her sorrow as she swore under her breath. She was closer to the kids than any of them. "Damn kids! Why would he do it?" She gestured helplessly again. "No, scratch that. This is just another stupid thing I've seen kids do over the years. There's always that moment where you know a kid is sinking and has suddenly changed. I always wonder what happened. We think of home first, but suddenly they're hanging around with different kids, or they suddenly dress differently, talk differently. They're not that same happy kid. Then there's the grades..." She sighed, and he could see how rattled she was.

"Jackson was like that?" he said.

She was shaking her head, thinking, and he sensed her vulnerability. For some reason, she was letting him see a side of her that he knew she didn't let anyone see. She settled her can of beer on the counter and then lifted her blue eyes to him. "Maybe that's why Rita Mae called," she said. "I thought it was quite odd, the questions she was asking..."

"Wait, Rita Mae called you here, tonight?"

"Yeah, right before you got here. She was upset, asked if I'd seen Jackson go into the closet. Then she asked about you..."

The way she said it had his eyes bugging out. "What do you mean, she asked about me?"

Anyone asking or talking about him or his family set him on edge, and the fact was that he didn't like being on anyone's radar. Tessa shrugged again just as he heard a knock on her front door. Of course, it had to be his brother. He knew it wouldn't have taken him long to get there.

"Don't look so worried, Owen," Tessa said. "She was just being nosy, is all. But she did make a rather odd comment as she was rambling on. She said nothing has come close to the mystery of what happened with your family until now."

She reached out and touched his arm, likely at the shock he knew had to be on his face. "It's just Rita Mae, Owen. It's what she does. I just hope your brother has more than one sit-down with her to tell her not to talk about the details of the investigation, because if there's one thing I've learned about her, it's that she knows far too much about a good many people, and she shares everything about everybody at the most inappropriate of times."

Then she was gone down the hall and was pulling open the front door, and he took in his brother, hearing his deep voice.

He was still stuck on the fact that someone was talking about his family, about their past, which no one in this town should have any idea about. As he thought of what he'd done, what he'd covered up, and what he hadn't shared with anyone, sweat broke out across his back, and that sick feeling he hadn't felt in years returned.

Chapter Seven

He'd stopped listening to what Marcus was asking, to the back and forth between him and Tessa. His brother had tossed him an odd questioning glance a number of times, but he no idea what the two had discussed.

Something about all of this was stirring unease in him. With this entire situation of Jackson, the kids, the school, and the pills, it seemed there was no logical scenario to explain who had provided the drugs. Finding the right answers meant they could close the fucking case.

And why the hell was Rita Mae shooting her mouth off about him and his family? What the hell did that have to do with Jackson Moore being found dead in a closet? This was just the kind of blindside he hadn't expected.

His arms were crossed over his chest, hands under his pits, as he leaned against the sanded-down wall in the kitchen. Marcus was jotting something down, notes, on a small pad of paper. It was kind of old school, but then, the sheriff's office still did things that way.

"So Belinda Lee and Hunter Rowse are Jackson's friends?" Marcus said.

Tessa shook her head, and he could see her frustration. He was kicking himself for tuning out their conversation so he could freak out when he should've been giving everything to them. He made himself pull in a breath and took in the way Marcus was watching Tessa. There was something about his brother that let Owen know Marcus wanted to have a word with him, too.

"No, he *used* to hang around with Belinda," she said. "I'm pretty sure she had no idea that his infatuation with her went beyond that of a friend, considering Hunter and Belinda were an item. Hunter and Jackson had been friends up until this year. Always saw them hanging out, and then they weren't anymore. It was just Belinda and Hunter. Then there was Petey Krantz. Saw him and Jackson together, hanging out a time or two. You should talk with all of them." She was thinking, considering, and from the way she was standing, he could tell how agitated she was.

Marcus was still looking at her. "Anything else you can think of?" he said.

Owen wanted to ask him who he'd talked to so far, and he also wanted to have a word with him about Rita Mae. "So I take it you have no leads yet?" he said, and Marcus dragged his gaze over to him. Owen knew that what he would say to him about the case in private and in front of Tessa would be very different.

"Talking to everyone again, is all," Marcus replied.

From the way Tessa was watching them, he could tell she'd picked up on something, and he angled his head at her.

Marcus narrowed his gaze. "Can I have a word with you?" he said before glancing back over to Tessa. "Thanks again, Tessa. If you think of anything or remember anything, call me, and, as I said, although you may have a lot of questions about what happened, because of the ongoing investigation, I ask you not to discuss any details." Marcus looked back at Owen and inclined his head toward the door.

"Tessa, I'll be right back," Owen said, taking in the confusion on her face, before he followed his brother to the door and outside, where his cruiser was pulled into the driveway behind Tessa's car. He took in the houses and his plumbing van.

Marcus lifted his shades from where they were tucked in his shirtfront and slid them on. "So, Tessa Brooks," he said. "Didn't know you were seeing her."

Owen picked up on something in his voice that said there was way more to his question. "We're having dinner, not getting married. Don't read anything more into it."

There it was, that amused smile on his brother's face. "Okay, Owen, whatever you say. So what the hell was that about? I could see you were thinking some pretty dark thoughts in there, and I'm pretty sure you didn't hear anything I said." So his brother had noticed.

"Just something Tessa said before you came. Rita Mae called her, questioning her, and she made some comment about our family and the scandal with Dad." He didn't elaborate more, as Marcus reached for his glasses and pulled them down, giving Owen everything.

"Excuse me?"

"Yeah, you heard me. You should have a word with her about not talking to people. Then there's the fact that she's asking about Jackson and the closet. She asked Tessa if she saw him go in. You know, that busybody kind of thing can create rumors, problems, and maybe even some false leads that could have your investigation going in the wrong direction."

The fact that she had brought up his family, his dad,

after all these years was what bothered him the most, though. Something about it had him wondering what the hell she knew.

"I'll have a talk with Rita Mae again," Marcus said. "She shouldn't be calling and talking with anyone. I'll make sure she understands this is a police investigation, not hers. It could be, too, that her and Tessa finding the body the way they did..." His brother looked around before shaking his head and making a rude noise.

"Rita Mae is the one who found the body," Owen said. "She screamed. That was the reason Tessa and I came running. You know, as we're talking about it now, I never thought to ask her what she was doing in the janitor's closet. She didn't say anything to you? Maybe we should compare notes."

Marcus hesitated. "How about you just tell me everything? Harold was the one who spoke with her, but you're right—why was she in the janitor's closet? Why is she bringing up our family and what happened with...with Dad?"

At the way he said it, Owen could feel that unease again. Everything about their dad should've been dead and buried, but it seemed as of late that things just wouldn't stay that way. "I don't know," he replied. "It was a long time ago, you know. She shouldn't be talking about it."

He wanted to pull her aside and find out what the hell she was doing and who else she was talking to. He shook his head and dragged his hand across the back of his neck.

"Go have dinner with Tessa," Marcus said. "Try to forget about what happened. I'll be having another word with Rita Mae to make sure she understands a boy's death doesn't give her leave to talk it up, creating drama and scandal. I'll shut her down. And this thing with our family...I'll make sure she understands that she's sticking her nose in business that isn't hers."

Marcus hesitated again, likely waiting for Owen to add something, but then he started around his cruiser, pulled open the door, and slid behind the wheel.

Tessa was walking his way, right over to him, barefoot on the grass. This was something else about her he hadn't expected. "So what was that about?" she said, gesturing toward Marcus, who was pulling out.

Owen took in how pretty she was. "Oh, you know, making sure he's not talking police business in front of you. I brought up the fact that Rita Mae may be leading him astray. You know, Rita Mae was the one who opened the door to the janitor's closet. Any idea why?"

Confusion flitted across Tessa's face, and then she shrugged. "I don't know. Why does it matter? Maybe she was getting something to help clean up."

Sure, that made sense. Maybe it was just the fact that she'd brought up the scandal of his family, something he wasn't comfortable with, that had him thinking there was more.

"Apparently, she insinuated that both of you opened the door together," Owen said. "But you and I know that when we heard her scream, we were still on the other side, in the bathroom."

Tessa went to say something, shook her head, and gave him the oddest of looks. "No, she must've been confused. This isn't because of what she said about your family, is it?"

He wondered how long she'd had the ability to look at him in this way, which had him feeling as if she could see something in him that no one else could. "You know what? Maybe we should stop talking about Rita Mae, and I'll help you with dinner," he said.

The way she looked at him again, he could see she wasn't about to be brushed off. "You're doing it again, Owen. You know how some people change as they get older? Well, you haven't. I'm more convinced than ever now that when you don't want to talk about something, you shut things down and change the subject." She lifted her hands and stepped back. "Fine, I'll let you have it tonight. Let's go finish dinner—but I have a question first." She was looking at him intently.

"Okay, is it one you want an answer to?"

This time, she couldn't hide the smile that seemed to pull at the edges of her lips. "Why is Rita Mae bringing up your family and something that happened so many years ago?"

For a second, he had to remind himself to breathe. "I don't know, Tessa. Frankly, that was another lifetime ago. It has no place in whatever demented gossip she's tossing out there about a boy who was found dead in a closet at school. You know, after Marcus shuts her down, I think I may very well ask her that same question."

All she did was nod and then gesture to the house. "Come on," she said. "I don't know about you, but I'm starving."

As he followed Tessa in, taking in the work in progress that she'd willingly taken on alone, he had to remind himself that whatever this was with her, at least now she wasn't openly challenging and fighting with him.

Chapter Eight

OWEN THUMBED THROUGH HIS PHONE, LOOKING AT THE text that something had come up and the plumbing job that should have filled his afternoon would need to be rescheduled. Fine with him, considering his morning hadn't gone as planned. He needed to check in with Marcus, he thought as he stepped out of his van at the diner he frequented for lunch.

The day was overcast, and he reached for his hoodie and pulled it on, glancing at the people on the street, the nods. He didn't feel like answering any more questions about the school, considering that was all that was on everyone's mind.

He pulled open the door to the diner and made his way to the counter, where he grabbed a stool and reached for the laminate menu. A coffee mug appeared in front of him, and coffee was poured, and he glanced up and took in Lori in her godawful mustard uniform, still pissed off.

He realized she didn't compare to Tessa. They were both blond and tall and slender, but there was something about Tessa: He didn't just want to spend time with her; she sparked his interest in ways no woman ever had.

"You're here for lunch?" Lori said.

Was he supposed to answer that? This was his go-to lunch place, and he hoped him and Lori no longer being together wouldn't have to stop him from coming. It was the perfect diner for him, quick, tasty, and within his budget.

"I'll have the clubhouse today," he said.

She scribbled it on a notepad, and he hoped that would be the end of it. "So I heard about the school and what happened to Jackson Moore. My sister was just over with the Moores, helping out, you know, with planning the funeral. It's a sad thing, what happened. Drugs at school... What were those kids thinking?" She settled her hand on her hip, ready to really dig into the conversation, though Marcus had already warned him not to talk about it.

"It is," he said. "Shouldn't have happened." He tucked the menu back in the slot and folded his hands together on the counter.

"So what do you think happened to him, and how did he get in the closet?" Lori said. "I know the Moores aren't going to stop until they have answers and someone pays for what happened. His father, PJ, said that he wants to know who supplied the pills. Any idea? You must have heard, or Marcus. You know how PJ is; he doesn't let it sit if someone wrongs him or someone he cares about."

There she went with the questions. Maybe he should have asked for the sandwich to go. He thought about the Moores, who did have a history of taking care of problems themselves.

"You know I can't talk about that—not that I know anything, anyway," he said. "There's an investigation, and I'm sure they'll find who's responsible and all those questions will be answered in time. Marcus doesn't disclose his investigations to me."

She still didn't move, and he wanted to remind her that he was waiting for lunch so she would put the order in, but he could see she still had something on her mind.

"You know, Owen, we never had a chance to finish our talk yesterday," she said, not pulling her gaze from him. Just yesterday, everything had been different, but he didn't want to rehash anything with her now, considering how she could go on and on. She was angry, hurt, and he didn't want to deal with her many emotions.

"Pretty sure we did, Lori," he said. "Look, I'm sorry, but you and I..." He just shook his head.

She stiffened, and he could see she wasn't going to make this easy. "Heard you and Tessa Brooks were out having drinks last night," she said. Now she sounded accusatory, and she hadn't even let him finish.

For a second, he didn't know what to say. He didn't have to ask where she'd heard that, considering no one seemed to mind their own business anymore. "We were at a bar, two people having a drink," was all he said. He glanced at her notepad, hoping this would be the end.

"So it's that easy, is it?" she said.

He wondered if he groaned. He wished his phone would ring or something. Maybe it was time he figured out a new place to go for lunch. "I'm not sure I get what you're talking about, Lori. We're done. Who you see is your business, and who I see is mine."

"Oh, I see, so you're moving on, dating, taking another woman out, when my bed is barely cold. I dropped off your box of things, but I expected you to call. I expected you to realize your mistake, not take out the first woman you set your eyes on. Is it really true about me and how easy it is for you to move on?"

Huh? "Lori, I'm confused," he said. "We're done, finished. In fact, how many days ago was it, right out there in that alley, that you told me to make a choice? In fact, you gave me an ultimatum. You want something more, and I'm not there—and you know what? I'm not going to get there, to the 'forever' thing. You made the right call, giving me that ultimatum. You can't force this..."

"You mean with me, or is this about Tessa? Are you sleeping with her?"

He knew people could hear everything, so he gestured for her to lower her voice. "Okay, that is completely not your business, Lori. Look, I like you, but there's nothing here with us, and there won't be. To be clear, we're done, and I'm not interested in picking up and starting something again. You were right about ending it. You deserve someone who can give you what you're looking for, and, just to be clear, that's not me, and it won't be me. You need to move on, find someone else, okay?" he said, more to end the conversation than anything else.

She gestured toward him. "Fine, got it. I'll put your order in." She ripped off the paper and slid it over the metal window to the cook in back.

He heard the door again, the jingle, and someone sat beside him at the counter. He glanced over, taking a breath of relief, only to see Rita Mae. Speak of the devil! Just someone else he wanted to settle things with, but having that conversation here wasn't exactly what he'd had in mind.

Rita Mae lifted her hand to Lori. "Lori, I'll have a coffee, please. I heard from Ellen that you've got this coconut cream pie to die for, so, since I'm on forced holiday today, I thought I'd treat myself to a guilty pleasure." She lowered her voice and leaned on the counter as if this were a secret, then let out a soft laugh as she took in Owen. "Hey, Owen. How are you doing today?"

What was he supposed to say to that? He wished now that he'd have thought through his need to revisit the diner he'd been going to for as long as he could remember. "Fine, great. You?" he said. He didn't really want to do small talk, so he lifted his hand to Lori. "Lori, make that order to go, would you?"

He glanced back to Rita Mae as Lori poured her a coffee and then strode away to deal with customers at the other end. It wasn't lost on him that she hadn't said anything about his order.

"Well, I've been better, considering I'm having to take the day off, and Marcus called to remind me not to talk about you know what." She actually made a motion as if zipping her lips, and he was pretty sure he winced as he lifted his coffee and took a swallow. "You know, I didn't mean anything when I called Tessa," she continued. "I just needed to talk to someone who was there. I still can't get the image of that poor boy from my head. You were both there, Owen. Finding that boy in that closet...it's horrible. I know we're not supposed to be talking. I get it..." She lifted her hands, then dumped cream into her coffee. He wondered what it was about her that made her blend into the background, someone he'd never noticed before.

"You know, Owen, going into that closet is one of the worst things I've ever done," she said. "Why did I go in there, again?" She looked up as if thinking. "Oh, yes, to help clean up the mess, to get a mop or something... That's what I told your brother, since there was suddenly a question about why I had been looking in there. At the same time, we all do things we wish we could undo. You understand, right?"

The way she said it had him giving her everything as he settled his coffee back on the counter. "Evidently, I don't, so why don't you spell out what this is about, Rita Mae? Sounds to me as if you're trying to hint at something. In case I need to remind you, my family is not your business. Not sure why you've brought up the local gossip about something that happened a long time ago. Like, what the hell was that about?" He lowered his voice, very aware of everyone around them.

"You mean when I called Tessa? Well, for one, she's my friend, Owen. You were out with her, getting drinks, after what happened and what we saw..."

He glanced away, spotting Lori talking to some old guy. What was this with Rita Mae? Was it a friend looking after a friend, or was it something else?

She pulled in a breath and gave him everything, and he took in the icy blue of her eyes, an odd shade. She seemed convinced of whatever it was she had to say. "You know, Owen, there's this thing about secrets. Everyone has them. Sometimes someone sees something and doesn't understand what it means. Think about it. Let's say someone saw something eighteen years ago, someplace in the woods—someone doing something that wasn't quite right. You wondering what I'm getting at?"

He felt sick, felt sweat prickling on his neck, as she leaned in and lowered her voice.

"I know what it is you did that night in the woods," she said. "You were burying something. I wondered why you'd be out so late, alone, at your age. What were you doing? But you know what, Owen? I consider us friends. We are, right?"

He couldn't get his tongue to move.

She reached over and patted his arm. "Kids today, huh?" She lifted her mug of coffee and took a swallow, and he couldn't pull his gaze from her as she settled it back on the counter. "You know, Owen. More than anything, you should know. Friends watch each other's backs and make sure nothing comes at each other." She slid around on the stool.

Down the counter, Lori had cut a slice of pie and was coming their way.

"Tessa is also a friend, a good friend," Rita Mae said. "I like Tessa and don't want to see her hurt. She's kind. Having someone who could pose a problem showing interest in her is something I don't want to see. Your brother's the sheriff, so let's just say that what I know is the kind of thing that could really hurt his chances of re-election. I just want to be clear, cards on the counter, so to speak." The pie appeared, and she glanced up to Lori and smiled. "Thank you, Lori."

Lori only nodded as she slipped his carton of to-go lunch in front of him with the bill.

He took it, pulled out his wallet, and tossed a twenty on the counter. "Keep the rest," he said as he stood up and shoved his wallet back in his pocket, then stepped away from the counter. He was still next to Rita Mae, who was shoving the pie in her mouth as if it were the best thing ever, and he waited until Lori strode away and Rita Mae looked up at him. "You know, Rita Mae, for a minute there, it sounded as if you were trying to threaten me."

She appeared shocked and set her fork down on her plate, shaking her head, giving him everything. "Really? Seems to me I was just clearing up any confusion before it could happen. Have a good day, Owen."

All he could do was take in this woman he'd known

forever from a distance. Panic licked the back of his throat as he thought about that night long ago, what he'd found, and what he'd promised himself he wouldn't share with anyone. It was a secret to protect his family, and he'd planned to take it to his grave.

Now, as he strode out of the diner without another word to Rita Mae, he had this awful feeling that her showing up at the diner had been deliberate, planned, as was her threat against him and his family.

He pulled open the door of his van and slid inside, tossing the Styrofoam container with his lunch on the passenger seat, and he stared into the crowded diner again. All he could think was that it was time he talked to Marcus.

As far as Rita Mae was concerned, her words had gone way beyond a simple warning. Could it really just be that she was concerned about Tessa, or was there something else?

Whatever it was, he couldn't take a chance on leaving it alone anymore. As he thought about everything that had happened as of late, with his siblings' questions about their dad, questions about what had happened, it seemed everything he'd thought was dead and buried was coming up in ways he couldn't control anymore.

Yeah, it really sucked sometimes, being the eldest.

Chapter Nine

OWEN TOOK IN THE HOUSE WHERE MARCUS NOW LIVED, across from Ryan's place, in a safe neighborhood. Charlotte's Subaru and Marcus's old pickup, which he never seemed to drive anymore, were parked in the driveway, and the sheriff's cruiser was parked in front. Jenny, Ryan's partner, was just pulling into her driveway across the street in her small Jeep, and she stepped out just as Owen did.

"Hey, you coming over?" she called out, lifting a paper bag of groceries.

He could see that Ryan wasn't home yet, and he shook his head. "Later. Have to see Marcus," he said.

Jenny walked up to the house and pulled open the screen door, and there was his niece. Right, he needed to find out what Alison knew about Jackson, the kids at school, the grad prank, and how any of that tied into Jackson being found dead in a janitor's closet. Then there was Rita Mae.

He started up to Marcus's front door, across the porch, hearing Eva, Charlotte, and Marcus's voices inside as he tapped on the screen door and stepped in. The living room was sparsely furnished, and his brother poked his head out from the kitchen at the end of the hall.

"Hey, didn't know you were coming by," Marcus said.

Charlotte appeared too. Her small baby bump was beginning to grow, and her deputy's shirt was untucked from her sweatpants. "Owen, could you tell Marcus here that he needs to take a break? I can't even get him to sit down and have a real meal." She slid her arm around Marcus's waist as Owen stepped farther inside.

Marcus was eating what looked like a granola bar, whereas Eva sat at the small dated table he recognized, which had to be a hand-me-down from his mom. It still had the scrapes from the knife Marcus had used to carve his initials underneath. He wondered if that was why his mom had seen to it that he got it. He realized they were both standing, looking at him, when he hadn't said anything.

"Marcus, you should listen to your wife," he finally said, then took in the exchange between them as if they'd figured out something was up.

"You know what?" Charlotte said. "Eva, why don't you give me a hand putting the laundry away?"

Owen watched as Charlotte held Eva's hand while they went upstairs, and he still said nothing, taking in the open kitchen.

"Okay, so what's going on?" Marcus finally said. Owen looked over to his brother, who was leaning against the island after shoving the last of the granola bar in his mouth, crumpling up the wrapper, and tossing it in the garbage under the sink.

"Heard you had a word with Rita Mae," he said. His hoodie was pulling at his shoulders, and his back was damp. He dragged his hand over his face, hearing the scrape of whiskers.

"You came over to talk about the fact that I had a talk with Rita Mae because of the heads-up you gave me?" Marcus said.

"Well, actually, I wanted to talk about Jackson and what you found, as well."

Marcus stilled for a second before leaning back against the island, saying nothing as he glanced around him to the front of the house. Owen could hear the distant voices of Charlotte and Eva upstairs. "You're asking me about an investigation? That's not something I would have expected from you."

He knew what his brother was saying. He was having trouble getting his words out.

"So what's really going on?" Marcus finally said. "Why are you really here?"

"I was having lunch at the diner, and who showed up but Rita Mae? Now, you know I would never interfere in your business, but there's something about that woman that isn't right. I'm telling you, she isn't sitting right with me."

His brother frowned, his brow furrowing. For a second, Owen wasn't sure whether he was going to laugh. "I think you may need to elaborate a lot more, Owen, because you're talking in circles, and this isn't something you normally do. Are you saying Rita Mae is still talking about my investigation even though I told her to shut her damn mouth?"

He dragged his hand over his face again and took a step farther into the kitchen. This was more difficult than he'd expected, finding the words to say what he needed to say. "Look, when Tessa said last night that Rita Mae had called and brought up our family and the case, I was bothered. But when she came into the diner today and sat down and started talking, it took me a minute to get my head around the fact that she wasn't just being careless.

She went out of her way to point out that she had gone into the closet to get something to help clean up the mess, which, sure, that's plausible. But why did she then bring up that she knows something about our family, about me, something I did?" He stopped talking, because he was staring at something he'd seen only a time or two in his brother's face.

Marcus took a step away from the island, looking out into the hall. Charlotte and Eva were still talking upstairs. He inclined his head to the back door, which led out to an enclosed porch still filled with junk Marcus had to deal with, things that had come with the house he'd bought. "We should talk out here," was all Marcus said.

Owen followed him out and closed the door before giving him everything again. It shouldn't have mattered, but it did, this privacy.

"This is something recent?" Marcus said.

How could he explain what he'd done so long ago? He remembered the night he'd walked downstairs after hearing something, remembered what he'd seen, what he'd known he had to do to protect his family. He shook his head. "No," he finally replied, and he could see the moment Marcus almost threw his hands up because he couldn't get the words out. "There're some things you don't know about what happened the night Dad left."

Now he had Marcus's attention, all of it. He didn't say a word, but those O'Connell blue eyes flashed with shock, disbelief, and something else. Marcus appeared about ready to grab him and shake him. "Owen, for fuck's sake, whatever it is, spit it out. You make everything painful with how you don't say anything. Did you do something? What the hell happened?"

Yeah, there it was. He'd touched that one nerve that was

still raw in all of them because the man they'd loved had been there one day and then gone the next.

"Look, you remember the office Dad had in the basement?" Owen said. "Well, I thought I heard something. It was late, everyone was asleep, and I got up and started downstairs. When I opened the door, light was coming from Dad's office, and Mom was just coming out. She'd been crying, upset, with blood on her hands, and she was shaking. I had never seen her so upset.

"She had this rag, and I just stood there, frozen. I didn't know what the hell had happened. She handed it to me. There was something in it. She told me not to look at it, to put it someplace no one would find it, to just get rid of it. I could see his office was a mess. Things were wrecked—the lamp knocked over, papers on the floor, pictures shattered. I didn't know what the hell had happened.

"She asked me again to help her, so I did. I went back upstairs and put my shoes on and snuck out of the house, grabbing my hoodie and a flashlight. I started running. I made it to that place at the edge of the woods where we used to go as kids, and I didn't think. The rag was wrapped around a knife, a switchblade. I buried it, the whole time wondering what the hell had happened."

He didn't think he'd ever get it from his head, the way his brother was looking at him in shock, horror. He just gestured toward him as he walked back and forth, buzzing with the energy that had suddenly broken free from a memory he'd been holding on to for so long.

"...What?" was all Marcus could get out.

"It was a secret," Owen said. "I never told anyone, but then Rita Mae brought it up at the diner as she slid around to me. She said we all have secrets, and she knows all about what I buried that night in the woods. The only reason I'm telling you is because she indicated her knowing what she does could hurt your chances of re-election, but all of this came up around Jackson Moore's body, the investigation. So I'm asking you, brother to brother, because of this, is there something in the investigation that could jam up Rita Mae, something that would make her use this to hurt our family and protect herself?"

He thought about Tessa. Was Rita Mae trying to warn her off of him, as well?

He wasn't sure Marcus was going to say anything for a minute. Then he seemed to pull it together and glanced to the door into the kitchen. Charlotte and Eva were still upstairs. "You buried a knife in the woods with blood on it. Dad's blood?"

All Owen could do was shake his head. "I don't know."

Marcus just stared at him before taking a breath as if trying to figure out how to deal with the fucking bomb he'd just dropped on him. "Now at least it makes sense why you're so against searching for Dad. What the fuck, Owen? What the hell happened? Why didn't you say anything? You kept this a secret all these years? ...Did Mom kill him?"

Owen glanced away for a second, then pulled his gaze back to Marcus. "I don't know what happened. I really don't. I was a scared kid, and I did it for us, for Mom. Did she kill him? I don't know what happened downstairs. All I know was that Dad wasn't there, and I've never seen Mom so upset. When I came home after burying that knife in a spot that will forever be burned in my mind, Dad's office was cleaned up, the mess put away. The next morning, Mom sat everyone down, all of us, and said Dad was gone. When I asked Mom later what happened, she wouldn't tell me. She said he was gone and told me to forget what I had seen. She said Dad wasn't who we thought he was. She said she needed my help to keep us together, that she didn't want us to know anything bad about him."

He'd listened to her cry for so many nights after, wondering what had happened downstairs.

Marcus pressed his hands to his face and then pulled them away as if trying to figure out how to come to terms with this, how to deal with this. "Rita Mae, Rita Mae..." was all Marcus said. "I wasn't focusing on her, but now I am. Why the hell would she threaten us like that?" He was thinking, then turned to Owen and said, "Can you take me to the spot you said you buried the knife?"

Owen just took in the brother he'd protected for so many years. "Yeah."

Marcus nodded, then rested his hand on the knob of the old door. "Let me tell Charlotte we're going, and then you take me there."

"And then what?"

"First, we find it, because if you're right and Rita Mae saw you that night, did she dig it up and take it, or is it still there? Either way, it seems now I've got two problems to solve, the murder of a kid and the question of how to protect our family."

Marcus stepped back inside and called out for Charlotte before turning back to him. "You know, you've held this secret for a long time, Owen. It's time that everyone knows, Suzanne, Karen, Ryan, and Luke. You have to tell them everything."

He knew what his brother was saying, but as he heard the footsteps on the stairs and watched as Marcus walked over to Charlotte, he dreaded going back to that spot. It had set in motion all he'd done since the night that had changed everything for their family.

Chapter Ten

THE SCENT OF ROTTING LEAVES AND DIRT AND THE SNAP of branches surrounded them as they made their way into the forest, to the spot he had run to in the dead of night. Even though Owen knew it well, he hadn't been back since that night so long ago.

Marcus still hadn't said more than two words to him since kissing Charlotte and then climbing in his van so Owen could drive. He knew this kind of evidence could stir up a world of problems for all of them.

"I don't understand why you'd bury a knife," Marcus said. "You ever heard of washing it, bleaching it to destroy the evidence, and then burning the rag? And I still don't understand how you didn't question Mom on what happened. You said you heard something, a fight—what else?" Marcus had transformed into the cop who wasn't letting anything drop.

"I was sixteen, Marcus. Seriously, fuck off, will you? Think back. I was a kid, a teenager. I had just started dating, just started shaving. I was protecting Mom, all of us. You want to bust my balls because I didn't think it through and hide the evidence better, go ahead, but I can't go back and change it. I wasn't planning out a crime and thinking through the details."

He took in the hill and the bushes, which seemed taller, and then the spot off to the right beneath a thick fir tree. "It's right here," he said, looking at the ground, trying to see the exact spot. He remembered how he'd used his hands then to dig through the tough ground, the fingernails he'd busted and the blood that had oozed from under them. Marcus had tossed a shovel in the back of his van and carried it with him now.

Owen reached for it. "Give it to me," he said. "You shouldn't get your hands dirty." He took the shovel and started digging.

"You sure about where you put it?" Marcus said.

Owen didn't look up as he kept digging. It shouldn't take that long until he found it, and he thought about the color of the rag: dark blue, stained with blood. Right, it would have been easier to clean it off, hide it, and burn the rag, but how the hell was he supposed to have known that then?

"I'm sure," he said, widening the hole and glancing up at Marcus standing there in his uniform, with his sheriff's badge and holstered gun, watching him and looking around. The perfect crime, he mused to himself, having the sheriff watch his back while he dug up possible evidence. He'd have laughed if the situation weren't so dire.

"You know, I've spoken with dozens of kids from the school today, and so has Harold, and Lonnie too. No one wanted to talk. I even had a few parents shut us down, ask us to leave, as soon as they had an idea that their kids could be implicated. I brought up the fact that one of the kids had already spilled about the grad prank, running naked around the school after popping pills.

"I'm going to have another word with Alison, since every one of the kids has suddenly gone mute. Never thought it would be that hard to get one of them to talk, but then, after seeing the shock on a few of the parents' faces when they heard the details of the prank their kids could've been part of, I suspect they wanted us out of the house so they could sit down with their kids one on one to ask them what the hell they were thinking. Then we add in the questions about Jackson and who was dealing the pills. Every one of them wanted to know."

Owen started widening his circle more, feeling dread in the pit of his stomach. "So what you're saying is that you've gotten nowhere on finding out what happened." He shoved the shovel into another spot even though he knew it was too far out. He hadn't buried it that deep, just deep enough that an animal wouldn't sniff it out and dig it up or the winter conditions wouldn't erode the dirt away and uncover it. At least he had known that much about burying something.

"Didn't say that," Marcus said. "Harold had a word with three friends of Jackson—Petey, Belinda, and Hunter. We've both been shut down by Belinda and Hunter's parents until later tonight. We've arranged to talk at seven when the parents are all there, and likely their attorneys, too, since news has already circulated that we're questioning the kids. Petey did talk to Harold, said he didn't know anything about the pills but that Jackson had been hanging out with Hunter and Belinda again. Said the two of them weren't really friends to him, just using him when they needed something, whatever that meant. I guess we'll find out what the other two have to say about that tonight."

He glanced up to Marcus, taking in the hole he'd dug

and how big it was. He knew his brother could see the problem.

"It's not here, is it?" Marcus said.

Owen shook his head. "No."

"You sure this is the right spot? Think about it, Owen. After all this time, all these years, you could be confused on where you put it. After all, it was a long time ago. You said yourself that you were freaked out, panicked."

He had a sinking feeling now that Rita Mae definitely had something on him, and worse, she'd had it all these years. Why? He had no clue why she'd done it.

He looked around, taking in the forest. To anyone, this area would look the same as the rest, but he knew it well. He pulled in another breath and tapped the shovel on the ground before he stepped back up and started filling the dirt back in. "I know exactly where it was. You're right, though. I screwed up. So I guess we know then, right? Rita Mae dug it up, but why hold on to it all these years?"

Marcus didn't say anything for a minute, just glanced away, something he did when he was thinking. "She was here, watching," he said. "She did say she had been watching you, right?" He just shook his head.

Owen didn't want to answer anymore. He'd already talked about the one thing he'd sworn he'd never talk about with anyone. "She said enough. She knows. Evidently, she's got the knife, and she plans to use it. Why? Maybe that's the question you should be asking," he said as he finished filling in the hole. His cell phone starting ringing, and he pulled it out, seeing Tessa's name on the call display. "It's Tessa," he said and pressed the green answer button. "Hi, what's going on?"

Marcus took the shovel from him and smoothed out the rest of the dirt.

"Was going to ask you the same question," Tessa said. "About…?"

She sighed on the other end. "Heard Rita Mae had words with you at the diner, and she called me again tonight. Look, she's always had this thing about you, about your family. I've known her for a long time, and I know how she can be about everything. Maybe I just wanted you to know that I don't feel the same way, in case you were wondering."

He would have laughed if he hadn't been standing at the scene of a potential crime, where he'd hidden evidence eighteen years ago as a wet-behind-the-ears teenager. "She was just being nosey, is all, warning me off. Maybe she thinks I'm going to mess with you in some way," he added, leaving out everything else. "So how did you know she had words with me at the diner?"

Marcus was listening as he held the shovel and gestured for them to go.

"She just phoned again and told me, but I also heard it from someone I know who was there, one of the other teachers. I guess they've had their own issues with her and kept their head down when they saw her pull up beside you. She can get pretty in your face, you know. She did come out and ask me if we're seeing each other, and she brought up your family and how I don't really know you. But I pointed out that having dinner together doesn't mean you're putting a ring on my finger or registering for china, so who I see isn't her business."

"So what are you doing tonight?" He couldn't believe he'd asked. For a second, there was silence on the other end.

"Getting the gutters up on the side of the house. You aren't asking me out, are you?" If anyone could lighten up a dire situation, he'd never have thought it would be Tessa.

"Well, how about if I swing by, give you a hand with your gutters, and then I'll take you out for a bite to eat?"

Marcus was now giving him everything.

"This doesn't mean we're dating, though," she said.

He couldn't fight the smile that pulled at his lips. "Absolutely not. It's just some home maintenance and then two people grabbing a bite. Be there in an hour." Then he hung up, seeing that Marcus had something else on his mind.

"You really think that's a great idea?" Marcus said.

"It's just dinner. I'm not about to let anyone tell me who I can and can't see."

Marcus inclined his head to the ground. "You know, Owen, you always were the stubborn one, but if Rita Mae has something, you really want to take a chance of provoking her right now? I'm the last one who would let someone threaten us, any of us, but until we know what we're up against, how about just lying low until I can figure out this Jackson thing and settle this issue with Rita Mae?"

He took in his brother, then glanced back over to the path before turning back again. "You know what, Marcus? At any other time, I'd likely agree with you, but the thing is that I like Tessa—a lot. For years, I've kept a secret and watched over all of you because I didn't know what else to do. No, I'm not letting Rita Mae tell me who I can or can't see. She's got some issue with me seeing Tessa?" He shook his head. "I'm not about to be scared off or threatened. So you go do your job, and I'm going to take Tessa for dinner, and then, when you have that sit-down with Rita Mae, I want to be there."

Marcus didn't say anything for a second. "Fine, go have your fun, but the minute Luke is back, you're telling everyone about what happened, what you did, and then the six of us are going to figure it out together. You're not carrying this alone, Owen. We're not kids anymore."

He knew what his brother was saying. "Fine, as soon as Luke is home," he said, then started walking until Marcus stopped him.

"But not before you and I talk to Mom," he said.

Chapter Eleven

THE WAY TESSA SMILED WASN'T THE FLIRTY KIND OF smile women often gave him. It was subtle, mixed with a ton of attitude, and he was starting to see she was doing her damnedest not to reveal it as she strode toward him, carrying two paper plates bearing corn on the cob, ribs, and potato salad, the takeout she'd insisted on picking up.

"Do you want to take a break and come down and eat?" she said, calling up to him where he stood on the extension ladder, screwing in the last screw of the gutter—which had seen better days, he noticed—with his cordless power drill. She was wearing faded blue jeans and a light green long-sleeved shirt with blotches of paint on it.

"All done," he said. "Can't believe you took this down yourself, but, Tessa, it's going to have to be replaced soon."

She stood at the bottom of the ladder, holding the paper plates, and he wasn't sure what expression was on her face. "You know, I didn't expect you to do all the work and put up my gutters for me," she said. "What you're putting up is way better than what I took down. My budget is limited, so I repaired what I could."

He sensed it again, that something, as if she felt she needed to defend her work. He tucked his cordless drill into the toolkit resting at the side of the house and reached for one of the plates she was holding.

"Wasn't criticizing, so don't take it that way," he said. "I know better than anyone that you work with what you've got. Just saying, you patched what you could, but you're going to have to replace it in the near future. You can patch something only so much before it's beyond fixing, and some-times there's nothing left." He didn't want to comment, either, on the fact that he'd basically taken over the gutter install and sent her to pick up dinner. "By the way, in case I didn't say it, as my lack of words has been pointed out to me, thanks for picking up dinner, considering I wanted to take you out."

There it was again, the slight pull at her lips, the smile he could see she was fighting not to let take over that pretty face. "Well, I didn't expect you to do all the work," she said. "I don't want to let you feel like the only reason I called you was to rope you into helping, because I'm capable of doing it myself. You're welcome about dinner—even though, funny thing, when I went to pay for it, I discovered you had paid over the phone." She gestured to him with her plastic fork before jabbing it into the potato salad. "Let's go sit around back. Sorry, by the way, for my lack of furnishings. Budget, you know. But here's a perfectly crooked deck that we can share."

He followed her around back, taking in the old deck, minus a railing. She sat on the edge of it, and he sat beside her, looking around at the yard, a decent size, overgrown in spots. It was likely on her list of things she'd be getting around to as soon as she could find the time. There was so much about Tessa he was learning now, having never had the chance to get this close to her.

"This is fine, Tessa—more than fine. You're building something here that's yours. So tell me, how come you're still single?"

She'd just taken a bite of her ribs, and there was sauce at the edge of her mouth. He couldn't help himself as he reached over and wiped it away with his finger. She flicked her gaze up to him, and he didn't miss the edge of awkwardness. Then she shrugged.

"I don't know, Owen. Just haven't met the right someone. Maybe it's a lack of time, or no one has interested me enough, or my standards are too high. Take your pick. I have other things, like this house, that take up a good amount of time..." She gestured again as she rested the paper plate on her lap and wiped her hands on her napkin. "I could ask you the same thing, Owen."

"Guess I could say ditto," he replied.

She raised a brow to that as she picked up a rib and took another bite, and he dug into his own. "There you go, not elaborating. You really don't like talking about yourself."

He wasn't sure if there was a question in there, so he said nothing.

"You know, I can't figure out what it is that has Rita Mae calling me about you," she said. "Before yesterday, she never brought your name up other than here and there, and now all of a sudden, after we went out for a drink and you were here for dinner, I'm getting the distinct feeling she's trying to warn me off you in one way or another, and I can't quite figure out why."

She gestured with her rib as she gazed up at him. From her expression, he could tell she was looking to solve a mystery, and he had to force himself to look out into the yard so she couldn't read anything from him. Damn Rita Mae! What was it about her that she felt this need to tear him down after all these years? It seemed now as if she'd been waiting in the wings the whole time.

He wondered what the hell Marcus had learned about Jackson and why he had the feeling there was something more going on behind the scenes that neither of them knew about.

"Not sure I can help you there, Tessa," he said. "How do you explain the inner workings of someone like her?"

He knew he was hitting below the belt, but he couldn't shake the feeling that Rita Mae was basically holding his balls in a vise and doing her damnedest to figure out how to control him and bring him down. It was humbling. He couldn't remember ever having been angry at someone like this before. When he glanced back over and down to Tessa, she was giving him the oddest of looks.

"Do you mind if I ask you something personal?" She rested her paper plate on the deck behind her and wiped her hands, and he couldn't help taking her in. He realized that every woman he'd dated, taken out, he'd compared them all to her. No wonder none of them could measure up.

"You can, but I'm not promising to answer."

She didn't smile, and another second passed before she nodded as if carefully considering what to ask instead of saying the first thing that could come out of her mouth. "Fair enough, I guess. What really happened with your family? I mean, Rita Mae keeps hinting at something, and I told you on the phone that she's always made comments here and there, but I never paid much mind. I only realized she had issues with you, but she's got issues with a lot of folks. When I heard she cornered you at the diner today and you left shortly after..."

There it was, more small-town gossip. He let out a sigh and finished off the rib, then took a mouthful of potato salad, giving himself some time to figure out what to say. He reached for one of the paper napkins and wiped his hands and face as he swallowed.

Tessa sat there so patiently and waited. Maybe that was why that edge he'd always felt with Lori didn't exist with Tessa. There was something about her; he could just sit in companionable silence, something he wanted more than anything.

"It's mostly gossip, you know," he said. "The thing about small-town stuff is that people see things and put their own spin on them. Yeah, she's a pain in the ass, but I left because my lunch was ready to go. She pissed me off, is all, considering Marcus had another sit-down with her to tell her to shut her mouth about Jackson's death. She doesn't understand discretion. That should say something, you know. As far as my family is concerned..." He stopped talking and shook his head, and all she did was reach over and press her hand to him, sliding it over his forearm. Her touch was welcome, and he didn't miss the way her gaze softened.

"You know what?" she said. "Forget I asked. You don't have to say anything. Rumors, gossip... You're a good man, Owen, even though it took a tragedy for you to give me the time of day."

It took him another second to understand what she was saying as she really looked at him.

"I think you've got that one backwards, Tessa," he said. "You were my first crush—until Steve Schwarkosky, that is."

There it was, the confusion. "What the hell are you talking about?"

Really? Did he want to talk about the fact that his good

friend had gone and asked out the one girl he'd secretly pined for after Owen shared his interest?

"Steve knew it was you I liked. After he asked you out, he told me he had shared how I had the hots for you, and you laughed and told him no thanks, then added that I would be the last person you'd ever consider going out with. After hearing that, my infatuation for you pretty much crashed and burned."

For a moment, he thought she was going to start laughing. She pulled her hand away. "Steve Schwarkosky was an arrogant ass. I went out with him two times too many. Yeah, he was quick to point out your shortcomings and told me you'd said you could do anything ten times better than I could. Was I furious? Absolutely, and I may have said something about how a jerk like that would never be on my radar."

He stared at Tessa, then glanced back out into the overgrown yard before giving her his full attention. He had to shake his head, because Steve was known for embellishing stories, and now he wondered if this was why everything between him and Tessa had felt like a competition. There was something about this moment, as if they could quickly slip back into the distance between them, to that place where neither would act on their feelings.

"Steve, Steve, Steve…" He shook his head. "Well, I guess I always wondered why it seemed as if you were trying to prove something to me, fighting with me, giving me the sharp edge of your temper. Now I know."

From the way she pulled in a breath, he could tell he'd hit a nerve. She glanced out into the yard and seemed to quietly think before giving him everything again. "Could say the same about you, Owen, always coming into a situation as if you could do it better. Every time I saw you, it was as if I could see what Steve was talking about. Did you really have the hots for me?" Amusement seemed to fill those blue eyes.

He leaned back on his hands on the deck. "Oh, yeah. There's just something about you, Tessa. No one can hold a candle to you. Damn Steve Schwarkosky! It seems he knew how to play it out."

Then he leaned in so close to her, and her gaze took in his lips. He pressed them to hers and kissed her softly, letting it linger until he heard his phone ring, and it was Tessa who pulled back.

He swore softly under his breath. The moment could've been awkward, but as he pulled out his phone, he saw Marcus's name on the screen. "It's my brother," he said, then pressed the answer button and stood up to take a step away. "Yeah, what is it?"

"Just finishing up and wanted to have a word," Marcus said. "You still at Tessa's?"

He glanced behind him to see Tessa sitting there on the edge of the deck, watching him. "Yeah, I am."

"Well, meet me at Ryan's, because we need to talk," Marcus replied, then hung up before he could add anything else.

Owen took a second with his phone and then shoved it back in his pocket, knowing playtime was over. He found himself pulling in a breath and letting it out, wishing... what? That Marcus hadn't called? That he could have more time with Tessa?

"You have to go, don't you?" Tessa said, though it wasn't really a question but more a statement of fact.

He strode closer to her, stood right in front of her, and held out his hands, and she slid both of hers into them so he could pull her up until she was standing. "I do," he said. "Timing sucks, though."

He angled his head, taking her in as she slid her hand over his chest. He rested his hand over hers and then leaned in and pressed a kiss to those lips again, which felt better than he'd imagined. Then he pulled back, taking a second to stand with her, feeling her heat, her closeness. Something about her seemed to settle him in ways he didn't think he could've explained to anyone.

"I'll call you," he said, then stepped away and started around the house.

She called out to him teasingly, "You make sure you do, Owen."

Chapter Twelve

Dark was starting to settle in as he pulled up in front of Ryan's house, seeing the sheriff's cruiser was parked back in front of Marcus's across the street. He stepped out of his van and took in Ryan's park ranger pickup in the driveway behind Jenny's small Cherokee. Both brothers were waiting for him on the front porch.

He looked right and left as he strode up the sidewalk. The door to the house was open, but Karen, Suzanne, and his mom didn't appear to be there.

"Mom had Suzanne and Karen over at her place tonight, considering Marcus is working on the case," Ryan said. "She has insisted we all show up at Marcus's tomorrow, though."

Marcus, who was still in uniform, said nothing as he stopped at the bottom of the stairs.

"So what's going on?" Owen finally said.

Marcus glanced over to Ryan, and for a moment, neither said anything. He wondered if Marcus had said something about their mom. Maybe his brother now knew.

"Ryan had a run-in with PJ Moore earlier," Marcus said. "You know, Jackson's father."

Owen waited another second as Marcus dragged his gaze over to Ryan, who was dressed casually in blue jeans and a faded shirt, with bare feet, holding a beer. He glanced back to the open screen door, and Owen thought he could hear a TV on inside.

"He's upset, rightfully so," Ryan said. "He had one of the kids from the school cornered, Petey Krantz. He had tracked him down on his ATV. Not sure all that was said, but PJ scared the crap out of that kid. He had him down on the ground, pinned up on one of the trails. Looked like he'd followed him or something. I don't know. He said he'd do his own investigation and wasn't about to depend on the sheriff's office here."

Owen looked from Ryan to Marcus and back. "Well, the Moores, as I've been reminded, have a way of finding their own answers and fixing their own problems. Was the kid hurt?"

Marcus gave him everything, and he wondered if this was why he had called him over. "Scared, more than anything. I need to stop on by in the morning and have a word with PJ. When I went over to Hunter's tonight, the parents and the lawyer were there. Apparently, PJ had a talk with Hunter, as well—you know, the kind of talk where he demanded answers and said the kid would find himself six feet under otherwise."

"And?" Owen gestured between his brothers, wishing Marcus would just spit it out.

"We know that Hunter Rowse's father is taking prescription pain pills, you know, opioids," Marcus said. "At the same time, they outright denied the opioid that Jackson took could be from those pills. The Rowses and their lawyer have basically pulled up the drawbridge to protect their kid. I did ask about the pills, and the father said they were all accounted for."

"But you don't believe him," Owen said.

Marcus shook his head. "Just something about people. You know that feeling you get when you know someone is lying? But it seems the family and the lawyer were interested in having me shift the focus somewhere else. You know, about the idea of running naked around the school, fingers are being pointed Alison's way. Hunter's saying it was all on her."

"Oh, it gets better," Ryan said. Now Owen could tell what he had been picking up on from Ryan: the tension of a pissed-off father who wasn't going to take this lying down.

"Was it her idea?" Owen said, looking at Marcus and Ryan, and then the door to the house opened again, and Jenny stepped out.

"She won't come down," she said. "She's still locked in the bathroom. Ryan, she's done a lot of things, but I know when my daughter's lying and when she's not. She's furious that someone would say it was her idea to run around the school naked, as if she could recruit a group of kids to do anything. She's the misfit, always trying not to fit in."

Ryan set his hand on Jenny's shoulder and let it run over her back. Without another word to his brothers, he pulled open the screen door and stepped inside, calling out, "Alison, come on down here!"

Owen took in the expression on Marcus's face. He was tired, pissed off, and maybe done with being sent around in circles.

"I'm not kidding, Marcus," Jenny said. "If she said she didn't do it, I believe her."

"I know, Jenny, but I still need to talk to her. These kids, all of them, are really beginning to piss me off, sending me in circles, pointing the finger at someone else. All we need now is for PJ to show up here because someone's throwing Alison's name out. The way this is going, someone else is going to get killed, and I don't want that on my watch. A kid died because of a stupid-ass prank—or was it something more? I don't know, but the lying and evading bullshit that's happening with these kids is making me think more than a few know what's going on. You should know Belinda also pointed the finger at Alison during Harold's visit there tonight. Her parents were also waiting with their lawyer, and she gave the same account, word for word.. Seems as if the kids and families got together to get their stories straight."

He heard footsteps on the stairs inside, and then the door squeaked open and Alison stepped out first, her face blotchy from crying and her mouth pinched tight with teenage attitude. She was barefoot in shorts and a bulky T-shirt, her arms crossed. Yeah, she wasn't giving in easy.

"Hey, kid," Marcus said. "I just wanted to have a word, you know, about the school prank. Why would kids be saying it was your idea?"

Owen didn't miss the way Ryan had settled his hand on Alison's shoulder, and she didn't shrug him off, though he wondered if her stubbornness would have her becoming suddenly mute.

"If someone's tossing you under the bus, kid, you tell us," Owen said.

Alison gave a deep sigh as she settled her deep brown eyes on him. "I don't know. I guess someone figured I'd be an easy target. My uncle's the sheriff, and my family's the O'Connells, so take your pick. I told you before that I heard what the kids planned, and I didn't want any part of it. I told them it was lame."

Ryan rested both his hands on her shoulders now, and Jenny dragged her gaze from Alison up to Ryan as if willing him to do something.

"So who told you about the plan to run around the school naked, and the pills?" Marcus said. He had a way of talking to her that was calm and reassuring but also said he expected an answer.

"I told you already that I heard it from a few of the kids, who said they'd heard it from Belinda Lee and Amanda Strickland. Hunter was also pushing the idea. Heard there was a meeting point right after school, behind the auto shop. There were a bunch of pills, too, that would be passed out, you know, a few of them, in a candy dish." She stopped talking.

"Come on, Alison. Spill everything," Ryan said. "What pills, and who was supplying them?"

Jenny was still standing there, her arms crossed. The expression on her face was one of shock, horror, or wanting to pull her hair out, Owen thought. Maybe she expected something more to crawl out of the woodwork.

"I don't know—everyone. You should talk to Hunter and Belinda, because I heard from Amanda that a bunch of the kids had gotten a hold of pills from their parents' cabinets, and Belinda had kept a tally of who was supplying what. Hunter and Belinda do everything together. They were going to put them in a bowl and mix them up, and everyone was meant to take one. No one would know who got what. Then, after they popped the pills, they were planning on stripping and racing around the school naked. They laughed about it. I said no thanks and came home. There's nothing else. You think I could come up with an idea like that? Organizing that requires the kids who run the school, the ones who can talk anyone into anything, and that's not me. I fit in about as well as Jackson Moore did." She gave that sulky look to her mom and then Marcus.

"So is Hunter trying to keep the spotlight from shining his way and Belinda's?" Owen said. "Tell us why he named you, Alison."

Alison turned to him and narrowed her eyes. He could see she was pissed off. "Hunter pointed the finger at me?" she said.

Okay, so they hadn't told her who it was.

She lifted her hands, and he could see she had that O'Connell fight deep within her as she shook her head. "He's lying."

"It wasn't just Hunter. It was Belinda, too," Jenny added.

Alison's jaw slackened, and she was fighting the tears that threatened to spill from her eyes. She forced another shake of her head. "They're damn liars! Now what am I supposed to do? How can they get away with this?"

She had every right to be upset.

"They won't get away with it," Owen said, jumping in, giving everything to Alison. "But it seems pointing their fingers at an O'Connell is the way they figured they could save their asses."

She dragged her fingers roughly over her eyes to wipe away the tears she was struggling in her fury to hold back. She sniffed loudly.

Marcus looked at his niece. "So how about you help us by telling us who we can talk to? Which kids would've been there, and who would know about the pills? If Belinda had a tally, who would know about it? Where can we find it?"

For a second, Alison seemed to consider something,

then said, "Amanda Strickland. Talk to her. I know she didn't supply any pills, but she always knew who did. You do know that prescription meds are passed around at school, right? They're easy to get. Everyone knows that. Amanda always said that if her dad ever found out about the candy bowls, she'd be shipped off to Kansas. I bet if you pull her aside without her dad around and let her think you'll talk to him if she doesn't come clean, she'll tell you the who and the why. And if she doesn't know, at least she can tell you where to find the tally that outlines who supplied the pills."

Ryan squeezed her shoulders and then pressed a kiss to the top of her head. "Just FYI, Alison, don't ever get any ideas about joining up with that crew at school, popping pills, or doing anything as harebrained as what they suggested, because if you do, I won't ship you off to Kansas, but your carefree life as you know it will suddenly have a serious kink put in it—like never having a moment alone, with every one of us poking our noses into your business at every moment of the day."

She rolled her eyes as if she'd heard it all before and then strode into the house without saying anything. The screen door slapped shut behind her.

"So now what?" Jenny said, gesturing to the brothers.

Marcus flicked his gaze over to Owen. "I'm going to stop over and see Amanda right now, have a word with her. If Alison's right, then I'll pay a visit to Belinda and then to PJ. I'm going to find out exactly what happened to Jackson Moore and how he ended up in that closet."

Chapter Thirteen

The clock was ticking as Owen drove back home. He'd left Ryan's, declining a beer and instead heading out just after Marcus, who had slid behind the wheel of his cruiser to go searching for answers and close this case, which he knew well would likely rock this community for years to come.

He still had to tell his family about the night his dad disappeared, and he could put it off only until Luke came home. It was a secret he'd pushed to the back of his mind and carried with him for so many years: his mom, her expression. Damn it all to hell! Marcus was insisting on sitting down with their mother first and making her bring up everything about their dad and what had happened.

He inhaled deeply as he flicked on his headlights, unsure why he had turned left down Tessa's street instead of driving straight home. He slowed as he started past, seeing the lights on inside the house, and he remembered his tools were still there. He pulled into her driveway behind her compact and stepped out, then started up to her door and hesitated only a second before knocking. Where the outside light should've been were only wires hanging down. Maybe he'd give her a hand there, as well.

The door opened. Her hair was damp from the shower, and she wore light knit lounging pajamas. "Hey...didn't know you were coming back," she said.

He stepped inside and then turned back to her as she closed the door. Something about her was different now; she was no longer the same girl who'd given him the gears and challenged him for so long.

"Realized I left my tools and didn't feel like going home to an empty house. Did I catch you at a bad time?"

Boy, that sounded pathetic.

She gestured toward the living room, and he followed her there, where a book was lying open on the green sectional with a blanket tossed over the back. "No, was just going to read for a bit," she said. "I can't remember the last time I got into a book. After sanding half a wall in the kitchen and vacuuming the dust, I decided I was done for the night." She slid around on the sectional and faced him where he sat on the end, his arm over the back. It was comfortable. "So what happened with Marcus? Or is it the kind of thing you can't talk about?"

There it was again, the difference between her and Lori. Why had he kept trying to settle on someone who wasn't Tessa? "He's trying to piece together the case and is getting the run-around from a few of the kids' parents, you know. They show up with lawyers and then point fingers somewhere else because they can."

She made a rude noise and shook her head without trying to fill the silence. She was absolute perfection. "Know it all too well. With some problem kids, you know you won't get anywhere, as the administration won't rock the boat because of who their parents are. Well, at least now I've got time at home to finish all this." She gestured around herself, not prodding him for more details. She didn't suddenly become shy or pull her gaze, just let her blue eyes linger on his. "You really don't like talking, do you, Owen? I guess I should be angry with Steve."

He took in the way her eyes flashed in amusement—and maybe a little anger.

"Ah, Steve... Whatever happened to him?" He couldn't remember anything other than that he'd received a scholarship to some community college. Last he'd heard, he'd done his first year in Minnesota. After that, Owen had lost track of him.

"No idea. I heard he changed specialties to become a veterinarian and met some girl in Idaho."

"Idaho, wow! Really, a veterinarian?"

She gave a smile and a soft chuckle. "So did you really come all the way over here to talk about Steve Schwarkosky?"

He shook his head as he reached out to Tessa and pulled her closer to him. "Steve who?"

Tessa went up on her knees and straddled him, sitting on his lap. He ran his hand up her back, feeling her perfection, and then he took in her lips, her face. He didn't say another word as he pulled her closer and pressed a kiss to her lips, taking it deeper as she slid her hands over his shoulders.

He ran his hand down over her ass, and she broke the kiss, slowly pulling back. She caught his lower lip between her teeth and pulled gently, teasing, oh so hot, and then she rubbed her nose to his.

"You came back for this," she said in a soft voice, low and sexy.

He brushed back her light hair, still damp in places, taking a minute to burn every part of her image into him. Her nose was perfect, her cheekbones high, and her brows were natural, as if she didn't need to put a ton of effort into primping. He ran his thumb over her lips and cheek.

"I didn't plan on coming back at all, but something had me turning down your street," he said. "I wanted to see you again." The way she was touching him, settling around him, he knew he didn't want to leave, but if she asked, he would. "God damn it to hell, Tessa—you are so beautiful."

A smile touched her lips again as she pressed those amazing breasts against him. "Well, if I said I'm glad you came back, what would you do?"

He knew what she was asking, as he somehow slid to the edge of the sofa and had her standing before him. As he stood up, towering over her, he shrugged off his hoodie and tossed it on the sofa behind him. He lifted her in his arms. She was so light as she slid her arms around his neck.

"I'd ask which way to your bedroom," he said.

As he gave her a little toss, she gestured down the hall. He strode down it, taking in the two bedrooms they passed and the one on the end, from which a soft light drifted out into the hallway. The small room was neat and tidy, and he took in the simple furnishings, the dresser, the mirror.

He settled her on the bed over the white duvet, and she just lay there on her back as he pulled his shirt off over his head and drank in her image. Then he moved onto the bed, holding himself over her. He lowered his head again and kissed her.

He didn't know what woke him as he blinked in the early morning light, with Tessa draped across him. Her legs were entwined with his, and her head was on his shoulder as if he were her pillow. Her arm was tossed over him.

He could feel himself stir again as he thought about the sex, which had gone beyond anything he'd expected. The way he'd touched her, the way she'd responded to him, the way he hadn't been able to get enough of her...

He heard the buzz of his phone and jerked up a bit, Tessa stirring.

"Didn't mean to wake you," was all he said as he gently freed himself from the sexy woman draped over him. He reached for his jeans on the floor, tossed in with Tessa's clothes, and pulled out his cell phone to see Marcus's number on the screen.

"You're calling rather early," Owen said as he stood up.

"Where are you?" Marcus said. "Because I'm at your house, and you're not here."

He sat back on the bed, and Tessa pressed her hand to the small of his back and rubbed. He glanced back to her. "I'm not there. I'm with Tessa," he said. At the question in her eyes, he let the phone slide from his mouth. "It's Marcus," he said, and she sat up. He took in those perfect breasts as the sheet slid away.

"Well, we got a problem," Marcus said. "I had a talk with Amanda last night, and, long story short, she said enough before her dad came out and started asking what I was doing there, just like our precocious niece said would happen. I gave Amanda the out, and she said Belinda keeps a tally of which kids supply which pills on her phone, in some app she uses. Apparently, though, Amanda was there. She said there were a bunch of pills, like ten different kinds, different colors and shapes, in pill bottles, and they dumped them in a candy bowl. Jackson was there, too.

"There were twenty-five kids, apparently. I got all their names. She said she'd taken one of the red pills, and she saw Jackson take a different one. The bowl hadn't gone all the way around the group before something happened. She said Jackson must've had some reaction, as he started foaming at the mouth and went down on his knees. He couldn't breathe. She said she ran, and Hunter said he'd get help, and everyone was freaking out. She passed out and woke up on her bed, hearing her dad downstairs, and didn't remember how she got home. I'm on my way to Hunter's now."

Owen pressed his fingers to the bridge of his nose and shook his head. "So do you know how Jackson got into the janitor's closet?" he asked. He could see that Tessa had figured out what he was talking about.

"I don't know," Marcus said. "I already called the lawyer and said I was coming over this morning. I plan on taking Hunter in. Wanted to give you the heads-up, because as soon as I finish here, we're talking to Mom."

So the case was almost closed, and here he was, looking in the eyes of a woman who had no idea what he'd done.

"Okay, thanks for the heads-up," Owen said. Then he hung up and reached for his jeans as he sat on the edge of the bed.

Tessa leaned in and pressed a kiss to his shoulder. "So you have to go?" she said.

The last thing he wanted was to leave, but at the same time, thinking of the conversation he needed to have with his mom was kind of a mood-killer. "Yup," he replied.

He turned and pressed a kiss to her lips, stuck on the fact that she hadn't asked him a million questions about the call. "So why aren't you hounding me on what Marcus wanted?" he said as he stood up and reached for his underwear on the floor. As he went to step into them, she took in all of him.

She shrugged as she scooped back her hair and didn't pull her gaze from his. "I figured you'd tell me if you wanted me to know, but as I'm well aware, it's an ongoing investigation. I'm not meant to talk about it. I heard you ask about how Jackson got into the closet, but I'm sure we'll find that out, right? Speaking of which, Rita Mae called me again last night. I didn't pick up, and she left a message, something about Hunter. She's always worried about Hunter. I guess I'd better call her, find out what that's about."

As he reached for his jeans again, stepped into them, and pulled them up, he said, "Why would she be calling about one of the students at school? Why is she so worried about Hunter?"

Tessa frowned and glanced up to him. "I thought you knew..." she said.

He stilled and gave her everything. "Knew what?"

Confusion crossed her face as she sat there in nothing, then shrugged. "Why, that Hunter is Rita Mae's nephew. Her sister is Angela Rowse, Hunter's mother. I thought everyone knew."

Upon hearing it, he realized everything made sense. He knew why Rita Mae had said what she had, and he also realized, as he stood there, that Tessa was watching him with a confused, questioning expression.

"Do you want to tell me what's going on?" she asked.

He reached for his shirt on the floor, pulled it on, and pocketed his phone, then took another second to pull it together. "I can't right now, but I will. Can you do me a favor?"

She said nothing, seemed to consider, and then shrugged. "Okay."

"Don't call Rita Mae back, not yet. Give me time to talk to Marcus. It seems my brother is likely going to want to have another word with her."

Chapter Fourteen

HE DIDN'T KNOW WHEN IT WAS THAT HIS FEELINGS FOR Tessa had changed. He still couldn't get it out of his head, what she'd asked of him, what had happened between them, between his stubbornness and hers and his unwillingness to be happy.

It had always been about making sure that his family was taken care of, that all of them were safe. Happiness for him seemed to have never been in the equation, or rather, he'd never allowed it to be.

He backed out of Tessa's driveway, dialing his brother again, though it kept going to voicemail. His mind was jumping back and forth over the fact that Rita Mae was Hunter's aunt. How the hell had he not known about that? She knew something about what Owen had done, but why was it coming up now? There was no such thing as a coincidence, so what exactly tied Rita Mae to Jackson Moore being found dead in the closet?

"Hey, you're not answering your phone, and this is really important," Owen said. "I need you to pick up..." He let his words hang, frustrated, waiting, knowing Marcus was likely in the middle of something with someone—Hunter, his parents, the lawyer? He didn't know. He heard the beep for the end of the message and swore under his breath.

He needed to shower and change, and he needed to warn his brother, so instead of going home, he turned the other way and started to the sheriff's office. Right, hadn't Marcus said that was where he would be?

Then there was Rita Mae. In some ways, she could very well be the catalyst for a scandal that would cause problems for his family, his mother, and Marcus, the kind of problems that could screw up everything for them. He felt as if he had been the one holding everything together for so long.

His phone rang as he drove, and he damn near landed on it, pressing the green button and seeing the private number, knowing it had to be his brother. He put the speaker on.

"What's going on?" Marcus said. Owen could hear voices in the background and what sounded like cars, too, as if he were outside or driving.

"Just found something out regarding Hunter," Owen said. "Did you know that Rita Mae is his aunt?"

There was silence on the other end, and he thought he also heard the police scanner in the background.

"No, I didn't," Marcus said. "You sure about this? Who told you?"

What was he supposed to say to that? "Yeah, Tessa told me. I guess she thought everyone knew. Just giving you the heads-up because you said you were going to see Hunter..."

"I have Hunter in the back of my car in cuffs," Marcus said. "His parents and lawyer are meeting me at the station. I've mirandized him, but he basically told me to fuck off, the little shit, and his parents, too. Had no choice. What I've got is weak, and the lawyer is already demanding to know the charges, as I've got only Amanda's statement, which was unofficial, as her dad doesn't know. Harold is already over at Belinda's. Haven't heard how that went, but hopefully he finds out about the app on her phone, the list of pills, or maybe she'll give us something on Hunter. Can only hope she's willing to toss him under the bus to save her own skin. But that would be wishful thinking, considering the lawyers are jumping into this and shutting it down."

He could hear his brother's frustration. "What do you plan on doing about Rita Mae?" he added as he drove. At the same time, his cell phone beeped with another incoming call.

"Don't know yet, but I'll be having a talk with her. Let me deal with the Hunter thing, and then I'll figure out Rita Mae."

"Just so you know, Marcus, with the threats she made and how someone dug up what I buried, if it was her, it could mean a world of problems for Mom, for you..."

Marcus cut in. "And for you, Owen. Look, I'll deal with it, but we need to talk to Mom today, so as soon as I finish, I'll call you. I've gotta go."

Owen's phone buzzed again, so he hung up and pressed the answer button. "Yeah? Owen here," he said before looking at the caller ID.

"It's Tessa, Owen," she said. "Rita Mae just called again. I know you said you didn't want me to talk to her, and I haven't, but she's going to keep calling. There's something wrong. I've never heard her so upset..."

He just shook his head, that sick feeling pulling like a knot in the pit of his stomach. "Yeah, something is wrong," he said. "At least now I know why. You know what? Tell me where she lives. I'm going to go see her."

There was silence on the other end.

"Tessa..." he prompted.

"Yeah, I'm still here. Why do you want to go see her?"

He really didn't want to answer. "She's neck deep in something here, and somehow, in all this, she seems to have taken issue with me. It's completely irrelevant, and I think it's time she and I sort some things out. It's likely best that you stay out of it. Whatever has happened, Tessa, I don't want you involved."

"Well, that's the thing: I am involved. Look, I'm not sure what her issues are with you and why she's stuck on some old scandal or what this is about, but if you're planning on going over there to see her, I'm coming too," she said. Then she rattled off the address, an area he knew well, only a few blocks from where he was.

"Thanks, Tessa, but do me one favor?"

He could hear her in the background as she pulled in a breath as if considering. "Okay, as long as you're not about to tell me not to come, because I'm on my way."

He would've smiled or laughed if the situation weren't so dire. "No, I wouldn't do that. I get it, but please just give me a few minutes with her one on one. Don't rush. Give me some time to talk to Rita Mae, just her and me. Because whatever this is that she has against me, I do want to settle it without her adding one more stab about my character and my family's. A long time ago, my dad left, and many people wondered what happened. The gossip was atrocious, the scandal, the accusations. I was a kid, but she wasn't."

He hoped she understood, because the last thing he wanted was for Tessa to hear how he had buried something eighteen years ago and his dad had never been heard from again. The knife, the blood, it was something he couldn't explain, and it would cast a shadow and open an investigation into something he wanted to shut down.

He willed her to say yes. There was so much to what had happened that Marcus was right about. They needed to sit their mom down and have a talk, but whatever it was that she'd done, he'd do everything he could to make sure she was left untouched.

"As long as you promise me that whatever this is, Owen, it won't come between us."

He pulled in a breath as he turned down the street, seeing newer homes, larger yards. He counted off the house numbers. "I'll see you later," was all he could make himself say.

He pulled up in front of the house, a new build with a red minivan in the driveway. Owen parked his plumbing van out front. He realized that this could make or break any hope of a future he had with Tessa. For the first time in what felt like forever, he hated someone, Rita Mae, who seemed to be the one person standing in the way of his chance at happiness.

Chapter Fifteen

HE LISTENED TO THE CHIME OF THE DOORBELL AND heard footsteps on the stairs before the door opened, and he took in Rita Mae's short red hair and round face. Her eyes were an odd shade of icy blue. She wore a white robe, and her hand went to her neck, pulling the robe closed, holding it. It took only a second for Owen to realize how rattled she was.

"Owen...ah, what are you doing here?" She looked around him, and he sensed annoyance, nervousness. He knew he was the last person she'd expected to see on her doorstep.

"Came to have a word with you. You mind if I come in?"

For a minute, he had the feeling she'd say no.

"Well, as you can see, this isn't a good time. I was just about to get dressed, and then I have to go out..."

He didn't pull his gaze from her. "This won't take long. I guess I can just stand here at your front door, then, and ask you why you keep calling Tessa, trying to warn her away from me. Funny thing about that little warning in the diner:

I couldn't figure out what the hell was going on with that threat you made against my family. Then I found out this morning that Hunter is your nephew, and he's one of the kids being questioned in what happened to Jackson Moore. Should we talk about this out here?"

He just stood there, then watched as she stepped back, the door open wide. She gestured for him to come in, and she closed the door behind him, then took a second with her hand on the doorknob before gesturing to the stairs, which led up to an open living room and kitchen. He walked ahead of her and took in the fireplace, the photos on the mantle, the furniture in blues and greens.

Rita Mae was still holding her housecoat closed with one hand, and he could see she was likely taking a minute to figure out what to say to him. There was that little issue of the threat against him and the missing knife and bloody cloth. Did she have it?

"You know, when I got the call for the plumbing emergency at the school, I remember you kept going on about kids and pranks and how you had been expecting something. I have to wonder about that now, considering what you said to me in the diner. I was a kid back then, but it sounds as if you're trying to hold something over me and my family."

She shrugged. "You'd likely go to all kinds of lengths to protect your family, wouldn't you, Owen?"

What the hell was he supposed to say to that? Of course he would, and he had.

"Don't answer that," she said. "I can tell by your face, your expression. Well, you should know that so will I. Kids do stupid things sometimes, all the time. You should know that better than anyone."

"So this is about protecting Hunter," he said, really glad Tessa wasn't there yet.

Rita Mae gave him everything and then pulled in a breath as she glanced away and strode around him, over to the kitchen, putting the island between them. She flattened her hand on the counter and seemed to study the laminate.

"I saw you that night, Owen, in the woods. Couldn't figure out why you were out there. It was late, and you were young. I was with someone..." She stopped talking, and he could feel the floor softening, stuck in that moment of D-day.

"Who, Rita Mae? Who were you with?"

She lifted her hand. "Doesn't matter. Let's just say I was out there and saw how upset you were. I saw you burying something..."

"And you, what, dug it up?"

She didn't smile but seemed to still as she pulled in another breath. "You buried a knife and a cloth with blood on it. It wouldn't have taken a detective to figure out that you'd done something, but I didn't have a clue what it meant. Then, next I heard, your dad had disappeared, left town, and no one knew anything. I was working then as an apprentice at the hair salon in town and heard the gossip and the stories. Lord, you have no idea. Everyone had a theory—that he'd run off with a mistress, that he'd done something and the law was after him. When no one heard from him, people said that maybe he was dead. Of course, by then I should have taken the knife in to the sheriff, but I realized I could be implicated, so I just sat on it. So did you kill your father, Owen?"

There it was, the one thing he'd never expected anyone to ask.

"Of course not," he said, but the way she was looking at

him, he knew she didn't believe him. If it had been him, he likely wouldn't have believed him, either. "So what does this have to do with Hunter? You want to jam up me, my family, Marcus? What exactly is your involvement in what happened to Jackson? Hunter had something to do with his death, and the other kids, with the pills."

She looked at him, giving him everything, and he could see she knew exactly what he was talking about.

"You know, Rita Mae, if it was an accident, why was his body in a closet?"

She shut her eyes and started pacing behind the island. If Marcus knew what he was doing, he'd have a few things to say, considering he was stepping into the middle of the investigation. But Owen wasn't about to let this woman twist the facts to hurt his family and shine a spotlight on something that had happened a long time ago and should've been left where it was, dead and buried.

"Kids panic, you know," she finally said.

He knew that well. "Is that what happened?"

"You know a lot about the investigation, but then, your brother is the sheriff. PJ Moore is not a man I want as my enemy, and Hunter is just a kid, just starting out in life. He shouldn't have his life ruined because of an idiotic choice. He wasn't the only kid there. He was scared, all the kids were scared, taking drugs that doctors prescribe like candy. He was panicked when he came and found me, crying, hysterical. He dragged me around the back of the school. Jackson was dead. The kids were all gone. They had left Hunter to clean the mess up. He's got a full-ride scholarship for Berkeley. He's got a good future, Owen. He shouldn't have to pay for something that wasn't really his fault. They were all to blame, including Jackson. He took the drug,

Hunter told me he started foaming at the mouth, choking, couldn't breathe. It happened so fast..."

"So if he died outside, how did his body get into the janitor's closet on the second floor?"

Rita Mae pressed her hands to her face, then wiped them away. "I helped him carry the body up," she said. "The school was deserted. The only teacher there was Tessa, and she was in her classroom, finishing up a lesson plan. I went in and distracted her while Hunter dragged Jackson's body into the closet. He planned on leaving. We both did. I was just downstairs in the office, grabbing my purse, and Hunter was waiting there, crying, freaking out still, when Tessa called down to say there was a plumbing leak, of all things...

"I panicked. I sent Hunter home and promised I'd take care of it. I never expected for this to evolve so quickly. I expected the weekend to come and go and for the body to be discovered only when the custodian showed up Sunday night. By then, I'd have figured something out. But I realized that was unrealistic."

He crossed his arms over his chest, hearing a car outside and knowing it was likely Tessa, but he didn't pull his gaze from Rita Mae. "So why did you really go in the closet? I could have fixed the pipe and been on my way."

She pulled her lip between her teeth, and sorrow seemed to settle there. "I don't know, Owen. I was panicked, freaking out. I knew I hadn't thought any of it through, because PJ would be looking for Jackson when he didn't come home. So I just did it, ripped the bandage off, and I hoped no one would come looking Hunter's way."

She pulled open a drawer behind her and lifted something out, a small box. She rested it on the island, staring at it, and then slid it over to him with her fingers pressed to the top of it. "That's the knife and the cloth that I dug up."

For a moment, he didn't know what to say. What was she doing? He walked over to her, to the island, and rested his hand over the box. "So why are you giving it to me, considering you've basically threatened to hurt my family with this? Then there's Tessa. You've made it clear you don't want me near her, but I'm not walking away. I've always had feelings for her."

He heard the doorbell and watched Rita Mae start. Of course she wasn't expecting anyone.

"That would be Tessa," he said. "She knew I was coming over. I told her to give me a moment alone with you first. She seems to think you have it in for me. I care about Tessa very, very much." He lifted his hand and settled it on the box again as if to make his point clear.

"I like Tessa and always have, Owen," she said. "Don't you hurt her—but I won't tell her." She gestured toward the box.

He couldn't shake the feeling that he'd just been given a reprieve, but he only nodded as she started to the landing to answer the door. "Who else was there with you that night, Rita Mae?"

She just stared up at him, and, for a moment, she said nothing. "Someone who's no longer in the picture."

He knew that was all he was going to get. "You have to tell Marcus what happened. Then there are the pills. You know that Hunter didn't supply them."

She stopped at the door and looked up at him, her hand on the knob. "No, he didn't, Owen. The people who supplied the pills were the parents those kids stole them from. That's who should be held responsible, but you and I both know that will never happen. It was an accident, a stupid accident. Who could've known an opioid could kill you?"

She seemed to consider something. "I'll call Marcus after I get dressed," she said, then pulled open the door.

He took in Tessa, casually dressed, gorgeous. She didn't have a clue about anything. What would he tell her?

Right now, he wasn't sure, but as he listened to the conversation in the background and glanced at the box in his hands, he realized the talk with his mother was a long time coming.

Chapter Sixteen

HE TOOK IN THE WOODSTOVE IN THE CORNER OF HIS living room, which he'd lit after he got home, and sat the small box on the table before he climbed in the shower.

Tessa was still at Rita Mae's. He'd kissed her and said he'd call her later, then left her there with her friend to talk about...what? He suspected Rita Mae wouldn't tell her what had happened.

Since then, he'd received a text from Marcus saying he'd be at their mom's in an hour.

He strode barefoot into the living room, his hair damp, wearing loose-fitting jeans and a long-sleeved black and white shirt. There, he opened the small box and took in the dried cloth.

He unwrapped the old switchblade and took it into the kitchen. In the sink was a bowl he'd filled with bleach, and he dropped in the knife, then strode back to the living room, where he tossed the box and rag into the woodstove.

As the flames took hold, his phone dinged again. He closed the stove and reached for it, seeing another text from Marcus: *On my way over to Mom's. Got a call from Rita*

Mae and just talked to her, but you already know that! Where are you?

He knew what his brother wanted, so he picked up his phone and texted back: *Taking care of something. Be there soon.*

He stood up, taking in the roaring fire in the woodstove, seeing the small box burned up along with the rag. In the kitchen, he lifted the knife and scrubbed, seeing all the blood flake off in the bleach. He washed it down the drain, rinsed off the knife, dried it, and shoved it in the back of the utensil drawer, with some old knives he never used. Then he washed his hands and rinsed out the sink.

He made his way into his bedroom and pulled on a pair of socks, then shoved his feet into his sneakers. In the living room, he closed the damper on his wood stove, seeing the flames flickering down to embers. He reached for a hoodie and his keys at the front door and made his way to his van, then climbed behind the wheel, feeling as if he'd cleared up one loose end that could have been a disaster.

He made the drive over to his mom's in less than ten minutes and pulled up in front at the same time Marcus did. He realized, too, that Luke's truck was in the driveway. As he stepped out of his van and took in his brother, who was giving him everything, he knew by his face that he was now running the show.

"You shouldn't have gone to Rita Mae's," was all Marcus said to him. Then he jutted his chin to the house. "Luke's home."

"Yeah. Rita Mae gave me everything," he said. He knew he didn't have to spell it out, so he said nothing else as Marcus pulled off his sunglasses and tucked them in his shirtfront.

"So she dug it up and had it, then?" Marcus said. "What did you do with it? And we are talking about...?"

He nodded. "Yeah, the knife, the bloody cloth. It's cleaned, burned, nothing left. I'm not that same stupid kid, so... I guess Rita Mae told you everything about her part, how she helped him get the body in the closet. What's going to happen?"

Marcus said nothing for a second. "I have to call PJ and tell him. Then I'll figure out what charges to pile on those kids. Every one of them played a part, but it could've been so much worse. Harold has Belinda on a misdemeanor with the prescription pills. It seems several kids were ripping off prescription drugs from their parents. Jackson picked a pill out from a literal candy dish that was being passed around. None of them knew what they were picking, from amphetamines to opioids. It's amazing, the pills that fill people's medicine cabinets. Jackson's reaction was quick. Then the kids ran when he died..."

Marcus just shook his head. "They really did leave it to Hunter to clean up. It's going to be a shitshow, with the charges. I figure a lot will plead out with community service. As for Hunter and Rita Mae, there's tampering with a body. Rita Mae is an adult, so for her it's a class-three felony. She did come forward, though. I'll talk with the DA."

Marcus didn't say anything else, and Owen wondered what he was planning to do. He was still having a hard time getting his head around the fact that he'd just been handed something that could've blown their world apart, but this time he'd made sure it wouldn't fall into anyone else's hands.

"Harold told me the idea to point the finger at Alison, according to Belinda, came from Amanda."

Owen just took in his brother. For a second, all he could think was how glad he was that his niece was a misfit instead of hanging out with those kids.

"Let's get this over with," Marcus said and started walking up to the door.

"You going to call everyone over now that Luke's home?" Owen said.

Marcus rested his hand on the front door and looked back to him. "After we talk to Mom and figure this out," he said. Then he opened the door and stepped inside.

Owen could hear voices in the kitchen: Luke and his mom, then her laughter. Dammit! He wished he didn't have to kill that mood.

He followed Marcus in and took in the surprise on his mom's face, her joy at seeing them. Luke had shaved, and his long hair, which he'd kept in a ponytail, was gone. Owen almost didn't recognize his brother. *Clean-cut and handsome. Holy shit!*

"So you're home for how long?" he said.

Luke just rolled his shoulders and took in the beer in front of him, and Owen wondered what that was about. "A bit," he said. "So what's up with you two?" He made a gesture of looking at his watch. "It's, like, not even the middle of the day. Don't you two have jobs?"

Owen's mom was giving him everything as if she'd figured out something was up. Just then, the back door opened and Suzanne strode in.

"Hey, you all! What's going on here? Saw both your vehicles out there in the middle of the day. Mom, I just spoke with Karen, and she suggested we pick up Jenny and Alison, as well, before heading out..." Suzanne was in the fridge, pulling out an Italian soda. She twisted off the cap, turned around, and took a swallow before saying, "What's going on here?"

All Owen could think was that this was no longer just a talk with his mom. This could be the worst thing imaginable.

"We came over to talk to Mom about something Owen told me about," Marcus said. "It happened years ago. We wanted to talk to just Mom, but we were waiting for Luke to get back first." He hesitated, running his hand over the back of his head, a motion he did when he wasn't comfortable.

His mom was watching him, and he could see the confusion, as if she didn't understand what this was. From the expression on Suzanne's face, he could see his sister had just figured out that their impending discussion could pose a problem.

"Should I call Ryan and Karen?" she said, holding her phone. Owen could see the alarm as his mom rested her hand over Suzanne's.

"No, don't call. I can tell just from looking at your face that this isn't just about dropping by to see how I am. Marcus, you know, don't you?" she said, then dragged her gaze back over to Owen.

Luke was watching him with intensity, and Suzanne was looking from him to Marcus, confused, as if waiting for someone to say something.

"I told Marcus about that night Dad disappeared," Owen said. "We wanted to talk to just you, Mom, but since Luke and Suzanne are here…" He gestured helplessly, because for a moment, he couldn't shake the feeling that he was betraying her.

His mom shut her eyes, and Luke pushed his beer away and narrowed his gaze. "What the hell is going on? You know something?" he said, sounding accusatory.

"Luke..." His mom reached over and touched his arm, a warning.

"Mom, I never asked what happened downstairs in Dad's office," Owen continued. "From the mess, it looked like a fight had happened. The knife you gave me had blood on it, and you wrapped it in a cloth and told me to get rid of it. I remember your face and how upset you were, so I did. I buried it in the woods. But then someone found it..."

"Holy fuck!" Suzanne shouted, her hands on her face. He didn't think he'd ever seen her so shocked. "What the hell, Mom?"

Luke said nothing, not pulling his gaze from their mom, who seemed unusually calm as she stared down at her fingers. "Who found it?" was all Luke said. Of course, he was ready to take care of whatever needed to be cleaned up. That was just what he did.

"Rita Mae," Marcus said, "but Owen managed to get it back and took care of it. He cleaned it up this time, so it's not as if something will come out now about it. We handled it. But the thing is, Mom, this has been an eighteen-year secret. Owen knew something happened, and he said nothing to any of us. Did you kill Dad?"

Owen wondered if he'd ever get the image of his sister's shocked face out of his mind.

"No!" his mom said. "Is that what you thought?" Her blue eyes flashed, and hurt came through in her voice as she pressed her hands to her face.

"Well, what was I to think?" Owen said. "Dad's office was wrecked. You gave me a bloody knife, and I hid it..."

"And did you see a body?" she said, cutting him off, leaning in. It had been a good many years since he'd seen that kind of fury in her eyes.

He hadn't, of course. No one said anything as they took

each other in, silent in the fallout of the bomb that had just been dropped.

"What happened, Mom? You have to tell us," Marcus said, his voice calm, reasonable.

Their mom sighed and glanced down at her hands. "This stays between us," she said before flicking her gaze over to Owen. "I'm sorry, Owen. I put this on you. I don't know what happened to your dad, and that's the God's honest truth." She lifted her palm in the air and shook her head. "Your dad had been acting strangely for some time, and I suspected he was involved in something I likely didn't want to know about. Men I'd never seen before had started showing up late, but that night, there was something different about it.

"I knew he was downstairs, and I knew someone had been there with him. I thought I heard something, not anything loud, just some noise that didn't sound right or didn't belong in our house. I'd been about to get ready for bed, and I went downstairs to his office and saw the mess— the broken lamp, the books and stuff knocked over, papers everywhere. It looked like a fight had happened.

"Then I saw the knife on that old wood floor, and there was blood, a lot of blood. I heard you coming down, Owen. I heard your voice, and I panicked because I didn't want you to see it, but you did. You saw the mess in the office. I grabbed an old handkerchief of your dad's that was there and wrapped the knife in it, and all I could think was getting you out of there, so I told you to hide the knife. I honestly don't know what happened or whose blood it was, because no one was there when I went downstairs.

"You did what I asked, and that gave me a minute to pull it together. After you left, I found a letter on his desk. It was in your dad's handwriting. I picked it up and read it, and it just said, *Goodbye. Don't look for me. I'm sorry.* That was it. I knew he'd left. The blood…" She shook her head. "I don't know whose it was, and I don't want to know. I realized then that I had never really known your father. He'd left me, left us. So I cleaned up the blood and his office. Owen, you never said anything, and I was grateful for that, but he left, and yeah, it wasn't easy. Maybe I thought he'd call or I'd hear from him, but I never did." She rested her hands on the counter.

Owen wasn't sure whether the shock he was seeing on Suzanne's face mirrored his. Luke said nothing, but he could see he was having some trouble getting his head around it, and then there was Marcus.

"So you never tried to find him," Marcus said.

"And where would I start? I had six kids! As I said to you all those years ago, it's just us now. He left us." She patted the counter again. "We should get going so we can meet your sister and Jenny and my granddaughter."

He could see his mom was still rattled, but he could also see her determination to shake this off as she turned back to him and took in Luke and Marcus, as well. Owen could see the way his mom had held it together for all of them.

"I see that you still have questions," she said. "You know what? I may have wondered for years, but I don't anymore, so if it's all the same to you, I want your word that Ryan and Karen won't know."

"Mom!" Suzanne spat. "You can't be serious. They have a right to know."

His mom stepped back from the counter and took in her daughter. "Do they? Now that I've told you what happened, can you just leave it be?" She reached for her purse at the back door. "Luke, there's hamburger meat in the fridge, if you could make up some patties for burgers tonight. Owen, if you can, pick up beer and wine for Karen. Marcus, Charlotte has been really tired as of late, so I told her I would pick up Eva on my way home and bring her over, and that way she can have a nap before coming over tonight."

His mom somehow managed to herd Suzanne, who was still trying to get her head around what she'd heard, out the door. The fact was that their mom had basically shut them down.

"So what are we going to do?" Luke said.

Owen just took in the now closed kitchen door of the house he'd grown up in. He shook his head as he stepped back. When his phoned dinged, he pulled it out and saw it was a message from Tessa: *Are you coming over tonight?*

He couldn't help the smile that touched his lips. He felt as if a weight had been lifted from him as he texted back, *No, thought you could come and meet my family.* Then he pocketed his phone and took in Marcus and Luke.

"Nothing, Luke," he said. "We're going to do absolutely nothing."

Chapter Seventeen

"So this is where you grew up," Tessa said.

Owen closed the passenger door of her compact. He still couldn't believe she'd talked him into letting her drive because his plumbing van, as she put it, was a work vehicle. He knew she was still trying to figure out how to get her head around Rita Mae's involvement, what the kids had done, and how senseless Jackson Moore's death had been.

"This is it. Thought you'd been here before?" he said.

She walked around the front of her compact, wearing a blue jean jacket, her long blond hair hanging loose, her face natural. Her blue eyes were striking. He slipped his arm around her and stopped for a minute before he leaned down and pressed a kiss to her lips.

"Nope, you never wanted to bring me home, remember?" she said teasingly. Whatever had been there between them way back, they had been doomed and just never happened. Damn. He was glad that he had a second chance.

"Hmm, well, just a warning about my family: They can be a handful at times, but we're a good bunch." He opened the front door, seeing surprised faces turn from the living room. His entire family was there, and he hadn't told anyone he was bringing Tessa. "Hey, everyone, this is Tessa. She's..."

Tessa raised a brow as she took him in, and no one said anything. He let a teasing smile touch his lips and could see she was amused, waiting for him to finish.

"She's my girlfriend," he finished, not pulling his gaze from her, for the first time feeling as if he wasn't all about his brothers and sisters. "Right?"

She pulled in a breath and rolled her eyes teasingly, then said in a low voice, "I suppose, Owen O'Connell. It only took you how many years?"

He thought he heard someone chuckle at her smart mouth, the hint of teasing she gave right back to him. He just shook his head as she shrugged, and he didn't let her go.

He kissed her again and linked his fingers with hers, then led her down into the living room, where his family was, knowing he'd likely hear about it all night, considering Tessa was the very first woman he'd taken to meet them.

It is better to keep your mouth closed and let people think you are a fool than to open it and remove all doubt.

Mark Twain

Chapter Eighteen

"Your phone has been ringing nonstop from inside," Tessa called up to Owen as she strode out below where he stood on her roof, patching a leak she'd discovered that morning after the overnight rain.

He was hammering in new shingles to replace the ones that were missing, and he pulled out the two nails he had held between his lips as he took in Tessa. Her hair was tucked behind her ears, and she was staring at his cell phone. He could hear the ringtone from where he was.

"It's Karen," she said, then pressed the answer button before he could say anything. "Hi, Karen. Yes, it's Tessa. Owen is on my roof right now, patching a leak for me..." She flicked her gaze up to him. So much about his relationship with Tessa was settling into something he hadn't expected. "Sure, of course." She held out the phone. "She says it's important and can't wait."

Of course it was, he thought as he tucked the nails back into his pouch and climbed back down the ladder to where Tessa was standing, one hand resting on the rattling extension ladder as he hurried down. He took the phone from her, seeing her curious expression. Just being here with her filled him with a sense of wholeness he hadn't even known he was missing. She said nothing.

"So what's so urgent?" he said into the phone before leaning down and kissing Tessa. She walked away with a smile.

"Owen, is there something going on?" Karen said. "And don't lie to me or blow me off or tell me it's my imagination, because I've picked up on something, and I thought it was about the kid who died, Jackson, but I just cornered Suzanne not less than ten minutes ago downtown, and do you want to know what she said?"

He slid the phone away, wanting to bang his head against the wall. "I have a feeling you're going to tell me," he replied.

He watched Tessa go back into her work-in-progress house, knowing she was still getting measurements together for the cabinets after having painted all the walls in the kitchen. He had encouraged her in his bossy tone, as she'd put it, to order the damn cabinets so he could help her finish the reno. She never pried about what he was thinking or feeling or what was going on with his family and him.

"You're damn right I'm going to! She said nothing," Karen replied. "But don't think I don't know when something is going on. I do, even though you hide everything. I called Ryan, and he said if there is something, he's out of the loop. Luke, well, you know him. He's not talking. Then there's Marcus, who used to spill everything, given time, but not since taking over as sheriff. I figure that has something to do with all the responsibility resting on his shoulders, running this town, protecting everyone, and dealing with the idiots who are causing problems. But you know what?"

He wanted to sigh again. "What, Karen?" He wondered

why he expected Tessa to come back out of the house. He realized that was something Lori would've done, hounded him in his face, asking a million questions about what Karen wanted, but not Tessa. There was so much she still didn't know about him.

"Although Suzanne can hide things at times, there's one thing about her that I do know. When she's acting strangely, and she is, I know something's up. I see her at Mom's with you and Marcus and Luke, whispering. I cornered her and got nothing, but for a minute, I know she wanted to spill. So this is how it's going to work: We're all heading to Marcus's tonight because Mom wants to make sure Charlotte has some time off her feet, so we're going to help plan the nursery for the baby and do whatever else Charlotte needs. After all, she's carrying the grandbaby Mom has waited forever for. We're going to meet across the street at Ryan and Jenny's first, and you're going to spill whatever this hush-hush thing is that has Suzanne so weirded out. Let's say in an hour."

He knew she wasn't asking. The bossiness in her tone told him she'd make his life and everyone's a living hell until they told her the one thing he knew his mom wanted none of them talking about. "You know, Tessa and I weren't coming until later, since we have a few things to do around here..."

"It'll keep," Karen said. "See you in an hour." Then his sister hung up.

Owen sent a quick text off to Marcus: *Just got a call from Karen. Been ordered to meet in an hour at Ryan's!* He waited a few seconds and then saw three dots.

Yup, same. Seems Suzanne's the weak link. See you there —and pick up the beer. I have to run to the store and grab more oranges for Charlotte.

He didn't know why he felt relieved, maybe because this was the first time in what felt like forever that he didn't feel as if he were carrying the weight of the family.

As he unlocked the ladder extension, let it slide down, and set it back at the side of the house, he took a deep breath. He strode into the house, taking in the fixer-upper at which he was spending more time than his own place, all because Tessa Brooks had stolen his heart.

"Tessa, we've got to go earlier," he called out. "I have something to talk about with my brothers and sisters."

Tessa was measuring a wall and turned her head, a pencil between her teeth. She let go of the measuring tape, and it slid back together. She pulled the pencil away. "Well, why don't you go, then, and I'll finish up here and meet you over there?" she said, another reason she was perfect. She was the least needy woman he'd ever met.

"Okay," he said. "Oh, do you mind swinging by my place on your way and picking up those books I got for Eva? Apparently, I have to grab the beer now because Marcus has to stop and get something for Charlotte."

From the way she shook her head, he could see her amusement. "Books for Eva—you really are a softy for that little girl." She walked over to him and slid her arms over his shoulders. She fit just perfectly, and he pulled her closer to him. "Of course I'll pick them up. Where are they?" She angled her head, and he leaned in and kissed her, running his hand over her butt before stepping back and slipping his hand in his pocket to pull out his keys.

"Living room, on the table. There's two, just came out. Charlotte said she loves these early readers about ladybugs, and I just happened to..."

She really looked at him as he unclipped his housekeys and set them in her outstretched palm. "Just happened to stop in a children's bookstore to pick up books for your little niece? You don't need to explain. I've seen you with her, all of you. You have a great family, Owen, and if I weren't already completely head-over-heels smitten with you, you'd have totally sunk me with the way you notice the little things like that. I know all of you are trying to make sure Eva knows she's not being forgotten. And, as you've said, this is a small town. The clerk at the bookstore mentioned to me how you made a point of having her search out any new books about ladybugs, so your secret's out, Owen. You're a hero to that little girl."

He rested his hands on his hips, wondering for a moment whether she was teasing him. All he could do was grunt, and she stepped closer and slid her arms around him. She hugged him and let out a soft laugh, and he pressed a kiss to her forehead.

"Hero, seriously?" He gave her an odd look as he stepped back, shaking his head.

"You can deny it all you want to, Owen, but I see who you really are." She stepped back and jabbed her finger his way.

Even though he knew she was teasing, she had no idea of the secret about his mom, and he wondered, if she really knew, would she still see him through those rose-colored glasses?

Chapter Nineteen

He left the beer in his van after pulling up in front of Ryan's, seeing Karen's practical four-door Honda also parked there. Then there was Suzanne's project car and Luke's pickup across the street behind the sheriff's cruiser. Evidently, he was the last one there.

He started up the walkway just as the door opened and Alison, wearing a pair of sweatpants and a baggy shirt, strode out in flip-flops Her brown hair was pulled back in a ponytail, and she was working a piece of gum.

"Hey, kid. You going over to Marcus's?" Owen said. He was about to rustle her hair but decided against it, considering the look she gave him.

"Mom's already there with Grandma and Charlotte," she said. "Dad kicked me out and said I have to go over now because of the adult talk I'm not supposed to hear, so what gives? You think I don't know something's up when you're all meeting over here? So what is it, a surprise or something, or is someone in trouble?" There she went, figuring out way more than she should.

"Just something we need to discuss, is all, and nothing

for you to worry about. Listen, I left a case of beer in the van. Could you take it over with you and shove it in the fridge? Oh, and I almost forgot—I picked up something for you." He pulled out his wallet and lifted out a twenty-dollar gift card for the little shop in town that carried all the fashionable jewelry and accessories Alison loved.

Her eyes lit up, and she practically landed on the card. "Thanks, Uncle Owen! So are you trying to buy my silence about something?"

He had to give her credit: She always thought some angle was being worked. "Not this time, but consider it an IOU for one," he teased. "I've got something for Eva, too. Tessa's bringing it. Don't forget to take the beer!"

He started up the steps, watching as his niece shoved the card into her pocket and then pulled open the door to his van. He was glad he'd thought to grab something for Alison, considering the books he'd picked up for Eva. He pulled open the screen door, hearing voices inside.

Marcus turned from where he stood in the kitchen. "It's about time you got here," he said.

"You're the last to arrive," Karen called out.

Owen took in Suzanne, who was leaning against the fridge, staring at her phone as if it held all the answers. Ryan leaned against the sink, still in his park ranger uniform, whereas Luke was in a white T-shirt and blue jeans, Marcus was in his uniform, and Karen, who'd called this meeting, stood in a navy skirt and a white sleeveless blouse. They all towered over her, as usual, but he realized there was something different. Right, her red hair, which was in a messy bun, now had a ton of blond highlights.

"Had to stop and get the beer because the guy whose turn it was suddenly couldn't," he said.

Marcus shrugged but didn't smile. "Cravings," he said.

"Charlotte can't get enough oranges right now. She ran out, so that took precedence over the beer."

"So what is this meeting for, again? I'm confused," Ryan said.

Suzanne didn't lift her gaze to him, still staring at her phone. She wouldn't look over to Karen, either. He could tell Suzanne wouldn't be able to keep his little bombshell a secret much longer.

"Well, I'm thinking we should put Suzanne in the hotseat," Karen said. "Or do any of you boys want to help her out and spill whatever the hell is going on?"

Karen had a way about her. He knew well that she wasn't about to let any of them blow her off or walk out without giving her something. She was just too damn good at what she did. But Suzanne... He'd never figured her for the weak link.

"I think you should tell them," Suzanne said. "I told you all that we shouldn't keep this from Ryan and Karen, and I know what Mom said, but it's killing me not to say something to Harold, either. Believe me, he knows me well enough to know there's definitely something going on. He asked me once, and I blew him off, saying it was nothing." She gestured quite dramatically at them, an edge to her voice. "But you know what? That didn't work. I can't have secrets in my relationship with Harold. I don't know how you all do it..."

He could see this would only go from bad to worse until she said something. He'd never have expected Suzanne, of all of them, to be this rattled.

"She's right," Marcus said. "They should know."

Luke hadn't said anything yet. He just stood there, the silent observer. Ryan, apparently, had just figured out something pretty bad was happening, and he was now staring intently at Owen.

"Someone say something," Karen said. "Who's it going to be?" She could be really bossy and demanding, and as she let her gaze land on Marcus, Luke, and then Owen, all he could do was pull his arms over his chest. "Owen?" she said.

Owen gestured over to Marcus.

"It really is Owen's story to tell," Marcus said, "but since he's kept it a secret for so long..."

"For eighteen years you knew something had happened to Dad!" Suzanne jumped in, cutting Marcus off. Owen could see how wound up she was. Karen and Ryan were giving him everything, and the shock on their faces said it all.

"I kept a secret, is all, Suzanne—to protect Mom, to protect all of us," he said. "I thought Mom had done something, but she didn't. Let's be clear on that."

Karen threw her hands up, and Ryan angled his head. Owen could sense the annoyance that was beginning to amp up between them all.

"The night Dad disappeared," Marcus began, "Owen went downstairs and found Dad's office a mess. Mom had a knife with blood on it, and she wrapped it in a cloth and gave it to Owen, telling him to get rid of it. He did, burying it in the woods, only he didn't realize someone saw him. Rita Mae was watching, and she dug it up and kept it. I know you all don't know everything yet about the death of that boy, Jackson Moore, because the investigation is ongoing, but she tried to jam up Owen and me, and our family. I can see by your faces that you're having some trouble with the details. After Owen and I went to the spot in the forest and discovered that Rita Mae must've dug up the knife, I insisted we talk to Mom, because..."

"I thought Mom had done something," Owen said,

jumping in, because he needed to shut this down. "She didn't, though. She told us. I mean, Luke, you were there when Marcus and I arrived, and Suzanne showed up shortly after. That's the only reason Suzanne and Luke know. Mom recounted what really happened. She was upset, horrified that I thought she'd done something. She had found a scene in the basement office, but no Dad. There was blood on the floor and a knife, and it looked as if a fight had happened. She said Dad was gone, and she found a note in his handwriting telling her so, saying he wasn't coming back."

Karen was leaning against the counter. In her shock, he knew she was having some trouble. "That's everything?" she said.

Luke, who had said nothing for so long, finally cut in: "Well...I'm not sure that's everything, considering one of the things Mom said was that Dad had people coming over for the last while at night, when we were in bed. She said something was going on, but she didn't know what. He wouldn't tell her. She was pretty sure Dad had found his way into something bad."

"She didn't say 'bad,' exactly," Suzanne said. "But she said she'd expected to hear from Dad, and when she didn't..." She gestured toward Karen and stopped talking for a second. "She didn't want anyone to know. She specifically asked us not to tell you and Ryan, even when I insisted. I'm still having trouble getting my head around how she could just not look for Dad..."

"Really?" Owen said. "Because I remember Mom explaining that clearly. She had six kids to look after, and she was basically gutted." Owen looked over to Suzanne, then dragged his gaze over to Karen. "I listened to Mom crying for I don't know how many nights. I know what it did to her. At the same time, for eighteen years, I thought she'd done something. I picked up the slack because she was doing what she could for us alone, and none of you made it easy. Now, if that's all, I'm heading over to your place, Marcus. We all need to go over before Mom and the others wonder and worry about what we're doing. She's going to ask, so come up with something. As far as telling everyone..." He shook his head. "You can't. I think you all know that. It was a close call with Rita Mae."

Ryan pulled his hands over his face and swore under his breath. "So you said Rita Mae had it and you took care of it. What does that mean, exactly? Seems there's holes here. Dad's office would've been a crime scene, with blood on the floor and a knife and only a note. No one here finds that strange? Where is the knife now, the evidence that Rita Mae had, and how did you get it back? Is this something else that we need to take care of?"

They were the O'Connells, and there was something about standing in this kitchen, just the six of them, that made Owen feel as though the weight on his shoulders had lifted. He could see the questions, though, that would likely always be there for each of them.

"I burned the rag and cleaned the knife, then hid it basically in plain sight," he said. "There's no evidence left. Yes, Rita Mae gave it to me in an attempt to do the right thing after what I can only imagine was an attack of conscience. So let's agree here before we leave that for Mom's sake, for all of us, this is the last we'll talk of this."

By the way Marcus was looking at him, he wondered if he agreed. "If any of this comes out, you all know my chances of keeping my badge are gone. Forget my re-election as sheriff. Suzanne, you can't tell Harold."

"But..." Suzanne started, but Karen reached over without looking and touched her arm, gripping it.

"Marcus is right, and so is Owen," Karen said. He could see she was taking a minute to get her head around it. "You can't tell Harold, just like Ryan can't tell Jenny, and Marcus can't tell Charlotte, and Owen can't tell Tessa. Because it's not just Marcus this could hurt. It's Owen, and Mom too." Karen let her gaze linger on Owen. "This stays between us. It has to—but at the same time, isn't anyone curious about what happened? I mean, it's Dad."

What was Owen supposed to say? He pulled in a breath. "You know what? For the first time since that night, I feel like I'm not having to keep an eye on everyone or pull you all out of trouble, so how about you do this for me? Leave it alone. I saw Mom's face, and I know what this did to her. That's something I'll always carry. If Dad was involved in something, we covered it up. I'm thinking it was pretty bad, and I, for one, really don't want to know."

He could see Suzanne considering, the way she was biting her lip. Karen, though, didn't pull her gaze from him, and neither did Ryan.

Luke shrugged. "Look, you all know I've looked, and I'm not about to put Mom through anything else. We have to drop it."

"Suzanne, you good?" Marcus said, and Karen tapped her arm again when she didn't answer.

"Fine, okay," she said, and then Marcus and Ryan started to the door, and Karen dragged Suzanne behind her.

Owen lingered a second with Luke. "You've been pretty quiet," he said.

Luke shrugged again as he playfully jabbed Owen's shoulder. "Said all I need to, but at the same time, between you and me, there's something about Mom's story that doesn't jive. I know there's more, but I guess letting sleeping dogs lie is what we do."

Owen just took in his brother, seeing that Luke thought deeply about a lot of things and was likely seeing ghosts where there weren't any, considering what he did in the army.

"So tell me about you and this thing with Tessa," Luke said. "Is it serious or not?"

He started to the door, picturing Tessa's sweet face. "You think I'd be bringing her around if it weren't?"

Luke inclined his head slightly, and an odd smile touched his lips before he gave a soft chuckle. "No, I suppose you wouldn't. Just so you know, I kind of like her for you."

He stepped out of Ryan's house, seeing his siblings ahead of them, heading over to Marcus's. Owen looked over to his brother, who rested his hand on his shoulder, and said, "You know what? I kind of like her for me, too."

Chapter Twenty

"I heard Marcus talking this morning with Charlotte," Eva said. "He said adopting me isn't as easy as it was supposed to be, and there're a lot of problems. Am I the problem, Alison? I don't want to be a problem. Will they still want me?"

Alison pushed Eva on the swing at the playground down the end of the street from their houses. There were a few kids there, mostly older because of the time of day, getting close to dinner.

The new kid at her school, a dark-haired boy named Brady, was across the playground, hanging out by the monkey bars. He was in one of her classes, and he'd never tossed her under the bus like some of the other kids, pointing fingers her way in the fallout of Jackson's death.

Yeah, she was still smarting over the fact that a grad prank could've come back on her, and she was still angry at those who had tried to accuse her, mainly Belinda, Hunter, and Amanda. Evidently, they had thought she was an easy target, being that she was aware of all the lies they had told, and they had ridiculed her one too many times behind her back.

Even though Belinda was now having to face the music, being charged for her part in the crime that had led to Jackson's death, Alison wondered whether she herself would ever shake that need for retribution. Anger was anger, and she still didn't know why she'd been such an easy target for them.

Then there was Brady, good looking and charismatic. Something about him had her giving him a second and third look, watching him where he was hanging out with Craig Lister, one of the jocks from school who'd never given her the time of day.

She pushed Eva again. "Of course they want you," she said. "Don't be ridiculous. You're not a problem. The only problem is all the hurdles Marcus and Charlotte are having to jump through, is all. That's what my dad said, anyway. Marcus and Charlotte will make it happen. Don't worry about it, Eva."

She knew, though, from listening to her mom and dad, that the problems with the adoption likely had something to do with the shooting at Marcus's house, when Eva had almost been hurt.

"Eva, if there's one thing I know about Marcus, it's that he knows how to fix things for all of us, and there's no way they're letting you go. You're our family. It's not you who's the problem; it's someone else making things difficult."

Who, she didn't know for sure. She'd listened quietly more than a few times when no one thought she could over-hear them, and she thought she'd heard mention of the state, the authorities, or maybe some bureaucrat.

"Charlotte and Marcus love you," she continued, "and

they'd do anything for you. They won't let you go. It'll be okay."

She looked down at the girl she spent so much time with. Eva was the little sister she'd always wanted. At the same time, she was still looking around the playground. She remembered how PJ Moore had looked at her while believing she had some part in his son's death. She knew he'd questioned most of the kids and threatened all of them, and she wondered when it would be her turn.

That feeling had her constantly looking over her shoulder these days, all because Hunter had pointed the finger her way and said running naked around the school after popping pills had been her idea. That wasn't how it had gone down, but a vengeful father couldn't hear the truth.

"Alison, does it make me a bad person to want to stay with Marcus and Charlotte? I love my mom, but she's in jail and won't get out for a long time. I still want to see her, but Marcus said I can't right now, and Charlotte said to just give it some time, and they'll keep talking to my mom and find a way to talk her into seeing me. Does she hate me? Is that why she won't see me?"

Alison held the chain, glancing at the little kids on the slide nearby. Eva jumped off the swing, and she took in her little face and her shoulder-length brown hair. She held out her hand toward her. "Your mom doesn't hate you," she said. "I shouldn't be telling you this, but I overheard from my mom and dad that Marcus tries every week to convince your mom to let them bring you to see her, but your mom loves you and doesn't want you to see her in that place. She doesn't hate you. Come on, squirt. Let's go before everyone wonders where we are. I told Grandma we'd be back in an hour."

Eva settled her hand in Alison's. She was dressed in blue jeans and a flowered long-sleeved shirt. They started walking, but she noticed that Brady had started toward them. Whatever he'd said to Craig Lister, she didn't know, because Craig was walking the other way.

"Hey, Alison," he called out.

"Hi, Brady. You live around here?"

He had such a nice smile, flirty. He was tall, lanky, and something about him had butterflies fluttering in her stomach. "Yeah, not far. You?" He dropped his gaze to Eva. "Hey, there. I'm Brady. I go to school with Alison. Are you her sister?"

"We live just up the street." Alison gestured toward their houses, then lifted the hand that was holding Eva's. "Eva's my little cousin. So you just moved here?" she said, looking down to see that Eva was smiling, standing so close, though she didn't say a word.

"Yeah, a few weeks ago, just me and my dad," Brady said. "My mom died a long time ago, so it's just the two of us. Don't really know a lot of kids here, but since we live so close, maybe we could hang out sometime."

That'd be great! "Sure, anytime," she said.

"Brady!" called a tall older man walking their way. He had threads of gray in his thick short hair.

Brady turned and lifted his hand. "That's my dad. Look, I've got to go."

Alison took in Brady's father, who looked right at her and Eva before dragging his gaze back to Brady. She hadn't seen him before.

"Been looking for you everywhere, son," he said. "Told you not to go far." He looked around again and then smiled at her as he stopped in front of them. "Hey, kids," he added.

She shrugged, holding Eva's hand. "Hey," she said.

"Dad, this is Alison, from school," Brady said. "Alison, this is my dad, Raymond."

There was something about the way he took her in. His smile didn't reach his blue eyes. For a moment, she wondered whether he'd say anything else.

He finally nodded. "Just Ray is fine, Alison," was all he said.

"Dad, Alison lives up the street, not far from us," Brady said. "Thought maybe I could invite her over."

Ray rested his hand on Brady's shoulder and just stared at him for a second as if considering something. "We'll see," he said. "Look, we've got to go. We'll talk about it later. Alison, good to meet you." He dropped his gaze to Eva. "And who are you?" he asked, really taking her in.

Instead of answering, Eva pressed her lips together tight, looking shyly up at him, holding tight to Alison.

"This is Eva," Alison said. "She's about to be my uncle Marcus's adopted daughter." She didn't know why, but the man seemed to really take in Eva, then nodded.

"So you're Ryan O'Connell's daughter?" he said, dragging his gaze over to her. Who was this man? The way he looked at her was so intense.

"Yeah, you know my dad?" she said.

The man didn't smile anymore, and he allowed his blue eyes to linger for another second before letting his gaze settle on Eva again. "It's a small town, Alison. Again, good to meet you. We have to go, Brady." He started to walk away, his hands shoved in his pockets. There was just something about him...

"Hey, sorry about that," Brady said in a low voice. "That's just how my dad can be." She wondered whether Ray could hear. "See you at school tomorrow!" he called out as he jogged after his dad.

She watched the man run his hand over Brady's shoulder and then rustle his hair, pulling him into one of those father–son hugs as they walked.

"How do you think he knows Uncle Ryan?" Eva asked as they started walking again, and Alison glanced over her shoulder, seeing Brady and his dad, Ray, walking the other way.

"I don't know. Seems my dad knows a lot of people. So remember, when we get home, you stop worrying about the adoption. It'll happen. You're a part of our family, Eva, and you're not going anywhere."

Alison didn't know why, but she was getting that weirded-out feeling that she couldn't shake again. It had her glancing back over her shoulder, but this time, she couldn't see Brady and his dad. Wherever they had gone, evidently, they lived somewhere close by.

Justice

THE O'CONNELLS

What will happen when the secret Marcus has been holding on to begins to unravel, and someone uses it as leverage?

One morning, Marcus O'Connell is confronted by his deputy, Harold Waters, about an accusation that he's hidden evidence of a crime. Harold knows something is going on in the O'Connell family. Even his partner, Suzanne, is acting strangely. Harold has made it clear that he doesn't do secrets, but Marcus isn't too inclined to share the details of the O'Connells' secret, even with Suzanne's urging.

At the same time, he learns that the sentencing for those involved in the recent high school crime has been assigned to an overtly conservative judge who makes no apologies for his bias, letting privileged kids walk while tossing others away all because of who their families are. Marcus soon learns there is much more going on behind the scenes with the judge than he's comfortable with.

Added into the mix is the fact that the adoption for Eva has suddenly taken a turn for the worse. Her grandfather wants to be a part of her life and is questioning Marcus and Charlotte's fitness as parents. With everything weighing on Marcus, he needs to make some hard choices about coming clean with his family's secret and taking a stand against the unfairness that has cropped up in a criminal case that should've been open and shut.

In finding a way to keep Eva in their family and close the adoption, Marcus may need to realize that carrying the

weight of the world on his shoulders alone isn't the answer
—and that reaching out, asking for help, and trusting
someone could be the only way to resolve everything.

Chapter One

At a knock on the open door to his office, Marcus glanced up, seeing Harold in his deputy uniform, his light hair cropped short, evidently recently cut.

"Thought you'd want to know," Harold said. "I was just at the courthouse and heard that Rita Mae and Hunter got off. Out of the twenty-five kids who were there, eight got community service hours. For Belinda, the judge added a charge of criminal possession of a dangerous drug, and she has a sentencing hearing coming up. Same with a few of the other kids, including Amanda. The sentences were all over the place, like nothing I've ever seen before. Did you have an idea that was going to happen?"

Marcus took in the file his deputy was holding, and Harold lifted it in the air as if it held all the answers. He tossed down the pen he had been gripping onto some notes on an open burglary case that had gone unsolved, then held his hand out for the file and leaned back in his chair. "What are you talking about? And what's in the file?"

Harold handed it to him. "All the notes regarding the investigation into Jackson Moore's death: the details of what happened, statements from every kid we talked to, the final list of seniors who participated in the prank and their roles, and the list of prescription meds, including which pills were supplied by which kids. You know, all the bullshit's in there, too, with the lies and the double talk and the finger pointing, the lawyers who wanted a deal, saying the kids didn't know any better and were just being kids. I've also noted how many were trying to implicate your niece, Alison, and the fact that just about everyone tried to lie their way out of it. Thought you might want a refresher before I tell you which kids are walking after making a deal with the DA and which ones got served with time behind bars."

For a moment, he thought Harold wasn't serious. He had to remind himself that joking around wasn't something Harold did. The man was quiet—and really fucking good at being a cop.

"There's one other thing you should be aware of," Harold said. "Rita Mae's lawyer is saying something about you."

That had Marcus leaning back in his chair, giving Harold everything yet again. His stomach knotted. "Excuse me...?"

Harold said nothing for a second, giving him a look that would've had suspects sweating.

"What the hell is she saying?"

"Something about you covering something up, you and your brother. She said there was evidence of a crime, and she gave it to Owen, and you knew about it."

He could feel his world unraveling.

"The DA isn't listening, though," Harold said. "He sees it as a desperate attempt to get a deal or something. It was Eileen, the assistant DA, who pulled me aside at the courthouse and asked if there was anything she should know about you or if there's any validity to any of Rita Mae's claims. I told her to fuck off. She knows you. But then..." Harold walked over to the open door. Out front, he knew Charlotte was manning the phones. He closed it and then pulled up the old wooden chair in front of Marcus's desk and sat down. What the fuck had just happened?

Harold took another second and then gave everything to Marcus. "You know I'm behind you one hundred percent, and you have my vote for sheriff. I've worked in a lot of different jurisdictions for some real assholes who didn't have a clue how the law works. I've seen commanding officers manipulate all kinds of laws to benefit themselves and their friends, letting one person off because they know the family and charging someone else for the same crime. But not you. I've seen how you go out of your way to be fair, even in this shitshow with the kids.

"At the same time, I know there's something going on between you and your siblings, all of them. Suzanne has about the worst poker face, and I told her I don't like secrets, but I've asked her twice and she's still not saying anything. When I heard this thing about the evidence, my first thought was to deny it, but as a cop, I know when someone is good for something and when I'm being lied to, and right now, I'm feeling as if I'm being lied to. About what?" He gestured toward Marcus. There was something in his blue eyes, the way he looked across the desk. Marcus could feel that this was the moment of truth.

There was no blowing Harold off, which was one of the reasons Marcus had pushed to give him the open deputy's position, which he'd had to fight city council for.

"So how about this?" Harold said. "You tell me to my face that there's nothing to this, and I'll drop it."

That was the one thing he'd never expected. He pulled

in a breath and didn't break the steely gaze being directed at him from across his desk. He pulled his hand over his chin. It would be so easy to lie. He was so aware of how happy Harold made his sister.

"I can see you're having some trouble explaining, and that only makes me more sure there's something here," Harold said. He leaned back, and Marcus knew he was quickly figuring it out.

"Everything isn't as black and white as you think it is," he started, but there was another knock on the door. The interruption was so damn welcome, as he was struggling to figure out how to blow Harold off and satisfy him at the same time—and maybe add in that this wasn't any of his damn business.

"Come in," he barked out just as the door opened. Charlotte was there, and he took her in. She was his wife, the love of his life, carrying his baby, and she also had no idea of the secret he was keeping.

She pulled in a breath. Evidently, she'd realized she was walking in on something. "Excuse me, Marcus. Just got a call from the Lees that PJ Moore is over there. All hell is breaking loose or something. He's got a gun and is threating Belinda, wanting the list of drugs so he can find out who supplied the opioid Jackson took, and he's not leaving until he gets it."

Marcus was already out of his chair, and so was Harold. "Anyone hurt?" He was at the door and knew his deputy was behind him.

"Not yet," Charlotte said, "but he's angry, as you well know, considering the DA wouldn't disclose the details about the pills, likely to prevent this exact situation." From the way she spoke, he could see she gave everything of herself to the job, to him. He took a second and let his gaze run over her, a moment between just them.

"Yeah," he said, knowing she understood that he didn't have the words right now.

He felt as if his entire world were beginning to break apart around him, exposing the secrets and lies and everything that had held his family's lives together. He lifted his hand and touched her cheek, then tossed Harold a look behind him. He knew he would keep asking until he got an answer, but at least now there was an emergency to be handled first, namely PJ.

"You want to remind me who the opioids were from?" Marcus said.

Harold said nothing for a second as Marcus let his hand rest on Charlotte's arm, then had her turned around and walking out of his office. He took in the empty desk where Lonnie usually sat, then the kid, Colby, who was neck deep in a file. Colby glanced up to him hopefully, and Marcus knew he needed to shut down the idea of him joining the action.

"You stay here," he said. "Harold and I will handle PJ. When Lonnie gets in, let him know I want a word with him."

Then he was out the door, Harold right on his heels. Harold hadn't said anything else, but Marcus was very aware that he wasn't about to let it go.

"I'll meet you over there," Marcus said as he headed to his sheriff's cruiser. Harold's cruiser was parked right beside it. He had his door open, about to get in.

"I mean it, Marcus," Harold said. "You may be my boss and the sheriff, but I'm damn serious. You're not blowing me off. I want to know, and now I'm more convinced than ever that there's something to what Rita Mae is saying. Keeping me in the dark isn't going to fly."

Harold climbed into his cruiser, flicked on his siren, and backed out, and Marcus did the same right behind him, gunning the engine to the Lee house, where PJ Moore was evidently keeping his word. The man was a vigilante. He wasn't going to back off until he had the answers he wanted —and his own brand of justice.

Everyone was taking the law into their own hands, it seemed. Then there was Harold and Rita Mae and all the fucking lawyers, and it seemed his ass was likely going to be hung out to dry. Just one more thing he needed, considering all the other responsibilities he had.

Maybe it was time he had another talk with Suzanne.

Chapter Two

HAROLD PULLED UP IN FRONT OF THE LEE RESIDENCE just ahead of Marcus. It was a two-story home with a circular driveway, and several people stood watching on the road and in the yards of the surrounding houses. He could hear yelling through the open door, and there was PJ.

He was a big man, maybe six foot five, he thought, and likely more than three hundred pounds of solid muscle. He wore blue jeans and a faded maroon shirt, and with his beard, he resembled a mountain man, the kind of man Marcus knew wasn't about to go quietly. Once he made his mind up about something, he wouldn't go down without a fight.

"PJ, step back now!" Harold called out ahead of him.

Marcus started up the walkway at a run. He could see a terrified Belinda standing behind her plump mother, who was looking freaked-out. Emotions were high, and PJ gave nothing to Harold, appearing unready to comply.

"PJ, step back!" Marcus shouted. "Last warning, you hear? This isn't how to handle this." He didn't take his eyes off PJ, who was now standing toe to toe with Douglas Lee, Belinda's father, a much shorter man.

"It's about time you got here, Sheriff!" Douglas snapped. "This crazy man threatened Belinda and us. We've asked him to leave over and over. I want him arrested. Get him the hell off my property!"

PJ didn't move a muscle or pull his gaze from Belinda, and another second passed before he lifted his hands and stepped back with a shake of his head and a murderous look in his eyes. Could Marcus blame him? Hell, no. But at the same time, he had to get through to him that his brand of justice wasn't going to fly.

"You going to come easy now, or do I need to cuff you, PJ?" Marcus called, his cuffs already out.

Harold stepped in, maneuvering Douglas Lee back. The man was still carrying on, and Belinda and her mom were close to hysterics. This had become a shitshow, just one more thing he had to handle, but all he could do was give everything to PJ as he dragged his gaze over to him. He was pissed off, angry. Yeah, he wanted heads to roll. It was there in the look he gave Marcus before darting a glance back over to Belinda, who was still standing behind her mother, terrified.

"You hear what I said to you, girl?" PJ said. "I asked you nicely. You and I both know that you know who supplied what drugs, and you know what my son took and who it was from. I want the names of the kid and the parents responsible for that drug, and I will have them!"

Marcus had his hand on the man's solid arm. "PJ," was all he said, and he didn't know why, but the man relented.

Marcus shoved his cuffs back in his pouch and led PJ away, over to the sidewalk, where his vehicle was parked at an angle, the door open. "You can't be taking matters into your own hands, showing up here and scaring the hell out of that girl and her parents. This has to stop, PJ. I know you want answers, and I understand the answers you want," he said.

The neighbors were still staring, their phones up, likely videoing everything he was doing. "Hey, you all! Show's over. Go on home now," he snapped. He was so tired of people standing around, gawking and taking enjoyment in the misery of someone who had lost a son. "Look, you can't be doing this," he continued. "We talked about this."

PJ was leaning against his car, his arms crossed over his massive chest. He was the kind of man Marcus would never want to go any rounds with, not anywhere. Cop or not, he never wanted to be on PJ's bad side. He was well aware people were still watching and listening despite his orders.

"You're telling me to stay out of something that is very much my business?" PJ said. "My son is dead because of a bunch of snot-nosed, privileged rich kids pushing their parents' drugs. Jackson wasn't into drugs. You know that. He was a good kid. What happened was murder. You know it, and I know it, and everyone who's responsible knows it. I told you I wouldn't sit on by and do nothing. I want answers for everything, and I've yet to get them. The DA tried to blow me off—and then there's you, Marcus. You know what I'm talking about. If the roles were reversed, I doubt you'd rest until you knew who did what. I want names, and I'm not asking anymore."

What the hell was he supposed to say to that? The man was completely right.

"Even if I agree with you, you know my hands are tied," he said. "Come on, PJ. This isn't the way. She's just a kid..." A stupid kid, he thought but didn't add. He needed another word with Harold to find out what was going on.

"She's not a kid," PJ said. "You and I both know the only reason she's scared now is because she was caught. You think she really gave a shit as she stood there and watched my son drown as he asphyxiated? She ran and lied, did everything she could to cover it up and save her own skin, just like every other kid who was a part of Jackson's death. He was dragged into a closet and left there, yet what's happening to the kids responsible? A slap on the wrist, or a few weekends spent picking up garbage. What about the kid who supplied the drug? You know who it was. What the hell are these parents doing, anyway, with all these drugs in their houses, the kind of drugs that can kill a kid?"

Marcus rested his hand on the roof of his cruiser. He didn't have to look over to see that most of the onlookers had moved back, but they were still there, listening to way too much and likely creating their own spin on what was going on.

"Look, between you and me, you're saying the same things I've said," Marcus started. "But there's a process, PJ. Justice will be served. You have my word…"

PJ looked at him with intensity and angled his head. "Bullshit, Marcus. If you've been following what's going on, you know that isn't justice. You have any idea who's getting time and who's walking? I've sat in that courtroom to watch thirteen kids go before the presiding judge, and you know what I heard? Eight of them, with their fancy high-priced lawyers, basically bought their way out.

"That pompous judge said, and I quote, that they were misguided kids who'd made a few bad choices. He said because they have great futures ahead of them, he wasn't about to penalize them and ruin their lives because of one mistake. He said a few other undesirable kids, kids that had come from broken homes, had clouded their good judgement.

"I'm not kidding. He came right out and said these snot-nosed kids have good families, intact families, with a mother and a father, and because of that, they would see the error of their ways. I'm not sure why he didn't come right out and say that he was letting them off easy because they're privileged, considering I've never heard such unapologetic bias before in my life!"

For a moment, Marcus didn't know what to say. He hadn't had a chance to find out everything from Harold because the situation with PJ had come up. He had to remind himself to remain objective. So that was what Harold had meant when he said Marcus would want some background before finding out which kids got which sentences.

"I can see you're having some trouble here, Marcus," PJ said. "I didn't miss how that judge, that asshole, sat up there and alluded to the fact that my Jackson was nothing more than white trash..."

He could see the emotion in PJ's face. Marcus had to remind himself that fair was fair, but it was sounding as if things were going sideways. "You and I know that's not true, PJ," he said. "We grew up on the same side of the tracks, so you know I don't believe all that. Look, give me some time to look into this, to find out why and how..." When PJ went to interrupt, he pressed his hand to his shoulder as he looked up at him. "And I promise I will look into it. You know me, PJ. I don't agree with what you heard. Let me talk to the DA, find out what's what, and I'll get back to you. You have my word."

A moment passed between them as he let his hand drop

and took in a father who had every right to feel the outrage he was feeling.

"Come on, PJ," he continued. "You and I both know that Jackson didn't deserve what happened, and I will do right by him..."

PJ seemed to consider his words for a second, then pulled in a deep breath that sounded raspy. "You just make sure you do, Marcus. The clock is ticking, and I'm not a patient man. I want answers, I want justice, and..." He paused but didn't pull his gaze. His voice was low, but in each word, Marcus heard his determination—and a promise that he wouldn't be blown off by anyone. "I will have the names of who supplied those drugs." He lifted his gaze and went to take a step, then gave everything to Marcus again. "Am I under arrest?"

Marcus wasn't sure it was a question. He knew PJ wouldn't fight him, and he understood that he meant every word he'd said. All he could do was shake his head. "No, but I can't have you showing up at people's houses. Belinda is having her day in court, and I'll handle this. You have my word."

He took in PJ, unsure of what he was thinking. The man turned and walked toward an older-model pickup, rusted out on the sides, that was parked in front of Harold's cruiser. He climbed behind the wheel, the engine rumbling and the wheels squealing as he pulled away.

Marcus turned to Harold, who was walking his way, taking in the truck driving off.

"So you're not taking him in?" Harold said in a low voice.

"No, he's been through enough," Marcus replied. "I think you need to fill me in on exactly what went on in that courtroom. I promised PJ I'd look into it. From what he said, it sounds like the judge is showing favoritism."

Harold turned and glanced over his shoulder at the Lees, who were by the front door, talking, still upset. "Sure. That was why I was coming in to see you. But at the same time, what do you want to tell the Lees about PJ?"

Marcus considered it for a second. "Nothing. Just tell them it's been handled. PJ will leave them alone. But he's a father who lost his son, and their daughter has some responsibility there, so they should show some understanding, some remorse, and maybe some empathy."

Harold only nodded as he glanced up the street to where PJ's old rust-bucket of a pickup was still driving away. "Fine, I'll tell them, and then you and I can sit down, and I'll bring you up to speed. Then you can level with me. I mean it."

All he could do as Harold started back up the driveway to handle the Lees was climb back behind the wheel of his cruiser. He considered it for just a minute before starting the car, pulling away, and calling his sister.

It rang only once. "Hello?"

"It's your brother. Look, we've got a problem."

There was silence for a second on the other side before Suzanne sighed. "You're talking about Harold."

He shook his head. She knew exactly what he was getting at. "The one and only. He's demanding to know what's going on, considering you suck big-time at keeping a secret. He was already suspicious, and now Rita Mae's lawyer is making noise..."

"Marcus, look. Let's just get it out in the open. This is Harold, and I love him, and it's killing me, having this secret. So, yeah, I vote to just tell him." She sighed again. "I told you all from the start that I can't do secrets, and I don't want to keep a secret from Harold. I can't. It's coming between us. I mean, are you okay keeping this from Charlotte?"

What the hell was he supposed to say?

"I'm the sheriff," he replied. "I don't tell her everything, and she doesn't ask. She knows I can't tell her some things." He knew he wasn't really answering. Every time he looked at Charlotte, he wondered what she'd say if she knew. "Fine, but if this goes sideways..."

"It won't, Marcus," Suzanne cut in. "This is Harold. If you want, I can tell him."

He was already shaking his head again. "No, you've done enough. I'll talk to him," he said, then listened to the silence on the other end.

"I'll see you at Mom's tonight?" Suzanne added. Ahead of him, PJ's pickup was stopped at the stoplight.

"Yeah, I'll see you later," he said, then hung up, seeing City Hall ahead, where the DA's office was. He knew exactly what his next stop needed to be.

He was still sheriff—that was, until all hell broke loose and he was forced to resign because he had helped cover up a crime.

In the meantime, as PJ turned right to head to the property he had just at the edge of town, an older rundown home, Marcus was stuck on what he had said about being white trash. It was the same label Marcus and his siblings had fought while growing up, never feeling good enough or equal, always feeling as if everyone were looking down on them.

He pulled in and parked at City Hall. He should wait to have a word with Harold first, but there was just something about all of this, and he feared it would end with the town being turned upside down by a man bent on vengeance.

Fair was fair, and so was justice, but it didn't seem as if either were going PJ's way. The last thing he wanted was PJ Moore ending up on the wrong side of the law or, worse, one of the kids involved ending up hurt or dead.

It seemed someone, namely the judge, from the sounds of it, was too interested in following the old adage about justice not being equal for all.

Chapter Three

Marcus tapped on the open door of the assistant DA's office. Eileen's dark hair was short, and her dark complexion was free of makeup. Her normally long nails, painted with the deep red she was known for, were cut short. She had on a cream-colored cardigan, and the way she leaned back with that look she had, he knew she had a thing or two to say to him.

She pulled off her reading glasses and tossed them on the desk after closing up the file that had been open in front of her. "Sheriff," she said. "Didn't expect you, but I'm glad you stopped by. Saved me from having to track you down. Shut the door, please."

He gestured to her when she went to stand, her expression unsmiling. "Don't get up," he said as he shut the door behind him, taking a second to gather his thoughts before she could start in on him about what Rita Mae's lawyer was accusing him of, misconduct, destroying evidence of another crime.

He realized he was walking right into the lion's den, so to speak. Maybe he should've taken a minute or a day before talking with her, but no one had ever been able to accuse Marcus of being a coward. He could feel the tightness squeeze in his chest as he turned around and took her in.

"I was just at the Lees," he said. "We were called in because of PJ. Should I give you two guesses as to why? Or maybe you already know why he decided to pay them a visit. He's not getting justice. I can understand his demand for answers about who the opioids belonged to. What the hell is going on, Eileen? Harold started to fill me in on how the sentences for these kids are all over the map, and then PJ tells me something about the judge showing favoritism. Even my deputy was trying to wrap his head around it."

This time, Eileen did get up and started around toward him. He took in her flat shoes and black pants as she leaned against her desk and crossed her arms but didn't pull her gaze. She wore a ring on her finger. Apparently, he hadn't heard that she'd gotten married.

There was just something about the way she could look at him as if seeing right through him. He never knew whether she was angry or just didn't like him. Then there was the fact that he was positive she knew his secret. It was unnerving, not something Marcus had ever experienced from a woman.

"Well, that's unfortunate," she said. "I do empathize with Mr. Moore, but he'd better get his head screwed on straight, because that won't be tolerated. You brought him in?"

For a second, he didn't think she was serious. Maybe his face showed his surprise. "On what charges? Hell, no. I'm not arresting him. He's a grieving father who lost his son, and he's getting a very clear idea of how screwed up the justice system is. Nothing about it has brought justice for his kid. Remember that's what this is about, Jackson Moore, who never even had a chance to live. From where I'm standing, I'm starting to agree with PJ. Did the judge seriously say that he wouldn't ruin those kids' lives because they came from good families? Did he actually insinuate that the choice they made to take part in that grad prank wasn't on them because of who their parents are? Are they automatically being given a pass? Are we still playing that game?" He gestured toward her, and he could hear the sarcasm in his voice.

"What do you want me to say, Marcus? I was completely thrown by the judge. Thomas Root is known for his overt conservatism. As soon as I heard he was taking the bench, presiding over this shitshow with these spoiled brats, I knew justice wasn't really going to be served. He has unapologetically used his influence to block de-segregation in the federal courts and the court of appeals with his brand of reach. You talked with all of the families involved, Marcus. You know which ones have the kind of money to afford a high-priced lawyer and buy their way out of trouble. They've likely donated a huge chunk of money to something the judge holds near and dear.

"Added to that is that those kids have the right color of skin and background, the right family names. That means something to this judge. And yes, for the first time in my career, I have broken this case down into categories: skin color, privilege, broken homes, economic class, and prior records, including the records of their parents, siblings, and uncles—you name it. That's all this judge is looking at. Do you want me to go on?" She was so matter of fact.

He couldn't believe they were having this conversation. "Jackson Moore is white," he said. "So does this judge care?"

Eileen pulled in a breath and pressed her hands over her face, then pulled them away. "The Moores may be white, but they're the wrong kind of white. You should know that, Marcus. At the same time, let me tell you, if Jackson had been a black kid who came from nothing, every one of those kids would likely be walking, because it seems no one is created equal."

He just stared at her, trying to get his head around what she was saying. "You know I wouldn't have allowed that to happen," he said. "I would've arrested and charged the kids the same way no matter who the victim was."

Eileen crossed her arms again and gave a heavy sigh before looking up to the ceiling as if he wasn't understanding what she was saying. "And, again, the charges would've been tossed out by the same presiding judge. Anyway, there's nothing I can do. My hands are tied, just like they were tied when the judge tossed an additional charge at Belinda Lee and Amanda Strickland, and six of the other kids. You know the Lees don't have the kind of money to hire a fancy lawyer.

"I don't remember a judge ever overstepping before as Judge Root has. He sees me as just a black woman. There's always been something with him. He's pointed out to me in private in his chambers that I should know my place, and that's not something I want to hear. If you're here to debate racial superiority and the fact that a judge is using his position to push his agenda and his beliefs, I agree, but it won't go anywhere. You can't take on a judge and win.

"You should know I already filed a motion to have Judge Root replaced for bias and prejudice, but you just missed my boss leaving my office after basically calling me on the carpet for daring to call out Judge Root as the racist prick he is. I was slapped back down. The motion was denied unanimously, and I was reminded that I had overstepped my authority by implying he's biased without irrefutable evidence.

"Everyone knows, by the way, that the man has spent a lifetime fighting to make sure courts remain all white, and he's made no secret of his beliefs in racial superiority. He believes broken homes are a blemish on society, and the right kind of people are the only way to keep order in a community. He stays, and I'll likely spend the foreseeable future handling bail hearings, being benched, and being pushed out. But, hey, it's all in the name of progress, right?"

Marcus didn't know what to say. He glanced over to the window. "So what is this about additional charges being tacked on?" Maybe he should've gone back and read the file, considering the kids involved.

"Well, other than a felony charge being added, I already know Belinda is looking at some hard time. The DA said the judge is likely going to give her five years. Six of the other kids, too. Your deputy has the details, but let me sum it up: Eight of the kids walked, with community service hours ranging from thirty to a hundred, with no probation. Six were given a felony conviction. Their only crime was not having the same last names and fancy lawyers as the others. They were given a ridiculous sentence, seven years, so two in the private juvenile facility before being sent for their last five in the adult facility. In case you're under any illusions about where this is headed, those private facilities are for profit only, not rehabilitation. I guarantee you a kickback was given, likely to the judge. Can I prove it? No."

She walked around her desk, and he could see how livid she was as she shook her head. "So buckle up, because the last round of sentencing coming up, I guarantee you, is going to be a fucking gong show. For the first time in my life,

I feel as if I'm on the wrong side of the law, considering the DA made a deal for Hunter Rowse, the one who actually hid the body and committed a felony, to walk."

His hand was pressed over his mouth, and he lifted it, not sure he'd heard her correctly.

"Yeah, my response exactly," Eileen said.

"No way," Marcus said. "He can't walk. He and Rita Mae dragged Jackson…"

Eileen was looking at him intently. "Right, Rita Mae, whose lawyer is the same as Hunter's and is screaming at the DA about something you've done. The DA seems to be on your side, saying that's impossible. He isn't listening. But then, you know Tibo Lewis. He doesn't want any scandal or problems in the sheriff's office right now. You know what, though? I'm asking you, because there's something there." She gestured quite dramatically toward him. "After seeing how this is blowing up, and we're seeing the kind of injustice that was common not even thirty years ago, something here isn't sitting right with me. Did you do something, Marcus?"

She leaned down on the desk, and he could see the fighter in her. She was scarred by the kind of ass-kicking that only life could dish out, the same kind of pain and hurt that he'd seen in his mother.

"You know what?" he said. "I did my job here, Eileen. I didn't hide any evidence in this crime. This is about Jackson Moore and a group of stupid teenagers who raided their parents' medicine cabinets, thinking it was a brilliant idea to pop pills, and then Jackson died, and instead of calling for help, every single one of those kids ran and is responsible. How is this being shifted my way? How about you focus on getting Jackson some justice—or should I be talking to Tibo Lewis about this?"

He didn't like being cornered or bringing up the DA's name, considering he knew the only thing Tibo did well as DA was flaunt his twenty-year-old bride, play all sides, and know exactly which calls to make for political gain.

"Go on, Marcus," she said. "You want to talk to Tibo, be my guest, considering he's deciding who's getting charged and who's walking. He's already clipped my wings, not wanting to ruffle the feathers of any sitting judge. You both speak the same language, so to speak." The way she said it, he felt the slap.

"Wow, really, the race card? Didn't expect that from you, Eileen. We've known each other a long time, and—"

"And we're, what, friends, Marcus?" she snapped, cutting him off.

"Nope, we're not, and maybe that's my fault, but I didn't see you reaching out my way, either. It's a two-way street. You know I've never treated you differently because of the color of your skin. I was raised better." He let his meaning sink in.

"You did something, Marcus," she said. "Whatever it is, you should know Rita Mae's lawyer's going to keep pushing until he gets a deal for her. She'll walk and won't get the obstruction charge that's on the table. Tibo is wavering, you know, and he sees himself in you."

He knew what she was referring to, but Tibo was twenty years his senior, distinguished, a member of the country club scene, to which he'd never be invited. They weren't the same. He could keep saying it, but there was a point where enough had been said.

"I'm not Tibo," he said. "Rita Mae isn't walking on this, and those other kids... No way. Then there's PJ. You know he'll never sit by and be okay with the fact that his kid isn't getting justice. He's smarting over what Judge Root said, as if his son doesn't matter." When she didn't say anything, he put his hand on the door and pulled it open.

"Marcus, I know you're not him, but at times like this, that's all anyone sees, and lines get drawn."

He turned back to her and took her in. "Maybe so, but I won't be picking a side. The only side I'm on is the one that sees justice served for Jackson," he replied, then started toward the door, still without a clue what she was thinking.

"Sheriff," she said, stopping him. "You make sure nothing will come back your way. And, just so you know, the opioids that killed Jackson Moore belong to Angela Rowse, Hunter's mother, for a back injury she had three years ago."

There it was, back to business. He knew she was giving him a heads-up because it would be only a matter of time until PJ figured it out.

"Thanks, Eileen," was all he said.

"I mean it, Marcus," she added. He rested his hand on the door frame, looking back to her. "I like you, but whatever it is that Rita Mae has on you, clean it up." She reached for her glasses and sat down in her chair. "Close the door on your way out."

He knew that was her way of telling him to go. She was damn difficult.

As Marcus turned the corner, he took in the DA ahead of him, speaking with another lawyer, seeing the practiced smile, the older charm. He went down the stairs and out the door.

Chapter Four

"You okay?" Charlotte said as she walked into the kitchen, sliding her hand over the small of his back and pressing against him so he could feel all of her.

He saw the time and heard a car door close outside. He still needed to change, and he needed to have a word with Suzanne. Then there was Harold, whom he couldn't keep avoiding.

"Yeah, just one of those days, you know." He leaned down and pressed a kiss to her lips, feeling the weight of the world. He took in her long dark hair, which was hanging loose, and her white cotton T over yoga pants, and he pressed his hand to the baby bump, his baby, who was growing bigger every day.

Charlotte was always touching him, and he realized now how quiet it was and how off she seemed. She was biting her lower lip. Yeah, something was wrong.

"Where's Eva?" he said.

"Guess you didn't see my text."

He went to reach for his phone as she sighed, something she did when she was holding on to something.

Since meeting with Eileen, he'd been trying to get his head around the PJ thing. Then there was the fact that Hunter had supplied the pill in question.

Charlotte put her hand over his wrist. "Don't bother. I'll just tell you. Change of plans: Everyone's coming over here tonight instead at Suzanne's insistence. Your mom had Eva today. She picked her up from school. She's also bringing Alison. I think they're stopping to pick up ice cream. I got a call from Karen because she couldn't reach you. Reine's father, Darryl MacDonald, reached out," she said. "He wants to see Eva before the adoption goes through."

He took in Charlotte and realized there might be more. She wasn't as calm as she normally was. Maybe that was what he was picking up on.

"I guess I wanted to talk without Eva here," she said. "Are we going to lose her, Marcus?" A tear spilled out, and she quickly swiped it away. "I mean, nothing with this adoption has gone smoothly. Ever since that incident at the old house, when that man died, it seems as if everything has come to a standstill. Problems that weren't there before suddenly exist."

It really felt as if everything around them had been spiraling, one thing after another, as if life couldn't just be simple and easy but instead was insisting on kicking him in the ass over and over.

He heard the screen door open before he could think of something to say. He was starting to get that feeling that something was in the works in the background.

"Marcus, I saw your car. I've been trying to get a hold of you." It was Karen, her heels clicking on the floor. She wore a black skirt that went past her knees and a white blouse, dressy, likely just from work, and she carried a bottle of white wine that looked well chilled. She sat it on the island and let her blue gaze settle in on him and then on Charlotte.

"I was just telling him you were trying to get a hold of him about Mr. MacDonald," Charlotte started.

Marcus found himself having to shove the Rita Mae shitstorm aside, and the weight of being sheriff, as he pictured a little girl he wasn't ready to let go of. Hell, no! He'd find a way to keep her or go down fighting.

"What the hell is going on, Karen? Reine's father wants to see her? I don't like this blindside. This simple adoption, which should've been done already, is having the kind of complications that shouldn't happen. Charlotte, we're not going to lose her," he added to his wife, who was looking to him to make things right. "Are we, Karen? Seriously, level with me as to what the fuck is going on, and do it before Mom shows up here with Eva."

He hadn't planned on snapping, but he could feel the edge of too many things he had to look after and handle.

"Look, I don't think it's anything like that," Karen said. "At the same time, the ask came not from Reine or her father but from social services, via her father's lawyer. I'm getting the feeling that something's not on the up and up. There's too much formality, which means someone's not comfortable. Something's likely in the wind. Look, have you talked to Reine recently?"

Karen had both her hands on the counter, next to the bottle of wine. Her hair was still red with blond highlights, pulled back in a tight bun, and he took in the ring on her finger, the flashing rock. He didn't know why he was noticing it now. He didn't remember seeing Karen or her husband, Jack, listed as lawyers in the Jackson Moore scandal.

"No, she won't see me," he said, "but I haven't tried in

over a week. I've been kind of busy, you know." He let his meaning sink in, knowing well that Karen understood everything that was going on behind the scenes.

"Well, I think you need to go see her, and do it now. This can't wait. You settle this thing and find out what's going on, because the adoption should've been done by now. The social worker's been dragging her feet, but I'm thinking there's more to it. So call Reine again. If she won't see you, find a way. Call in favors, whatever you need to do to go and see her, Marcus." His sister gave him everything, direct, to the point, then dragged her gaze over to Charlotte. "And, Charlotte, I think it would help Reine to see you, as well, so she understands how important Eva is to both of you and knows that even with the baby coming, she's very much wanted."

Charlotte was giving him everything, and he ran his hand over her shoulder, lifted her hair, and touched her cheek. She shrugged. "I think that's for the best. Do you think that's what this is about?" She gave everything to Karen. "I mean, that's silly. How could we consider tossing Eva aside? She's ours, our daughter, just like this baby."

Marcus pulled Charlotte in closer. "I'm sure it's not, but in case it is, yeah, we'll talk to her."

Karen went over to the kitchen cupboard, where the wineglasses were, and strode back to the island to set one down and twist off the bottlecap. "And, just so you know, if you have trouble getting in or she won't see you, I can get in, as her lawyer. But do you really want me to handle this when you need to sit across from her, face to face, and find out what the issue is?"

He knew what his sister was saying. He heard more cars outside, doors being closed, voices, and knew his family was about to invade their quiet house.

"I'll handle it," he said to Karen, then lowered his gaze to Charlotte. She settled into his arms again, and he ran his hands over her, trying to at least put a smile back on her face even though he still couldn't shake the feeling that everything was unraveling. "I will. Don't worry. She's ours, okay?" he said to Charlotte, wishing it could be that easy.

He pulled her closer and kissed her again before looking up to see Suzanne coming in, followed by Harold, who was carrying a case of beer. His sister's eyes were wide, and he knew that panicked look well. Evidently, Harold wasn't going quietly into the night. Time was up.

Harold was giving him everything, still dressed in his deputy's uniform, his gun holstered. From the way he walked toward him, Marcus could tell he wasn't willing to wait a moment longer.

He nodded to Harold and stepped away from Charlotte, letting his hand fall away as he took in the rest of his family coming in. Eva raced his way, wearing pink and white, and he lifted her and kissed her. "Hey, you! How was school? You have fun with your grandma?"

"Yeah, Mrs. Kramer brought in a pet lizard, and Patrick Turner let it out, and it ran under the bookcase, and we couldn't get it out, and there was screaming, and the principal came in, and the janitor got it out with a stick and a net..."

Right, it seemed nothing had changed since he'd gone to school. He put her down and ruffled her short brown hair, seeing her front tooth missing. Charlotte had played the Tooth Fairy and left two quarters under her pillow. She really did handle everything for them.

"Sounds like there was some excitement." He tilted his head to the kitchen, where Charlotte was, and said, "Go on and check in with Charlotte, okay?"

Just then, his niece, Alison, walked past and gave him one of her looks, not a smile, and he spotted his mom, who was shaking her head in a way that said there was evidently some teenage drama occurring that he'd best steer clear of.

Meanwhile, Harold was already out the front door and was looking back to him. Marcus took another second before pulling in a breath and following him out. Across the street, Jenny was on her way over, but Ryan didn't appear to be home yet. Luke was gone again, and Tessa and Owen would likely be there shortly.

"So is this you blowing me off or you coming clean?" Harold started. "Because Suzanne..."

"Look, I know Suzanne doesn't agree with us not having shared this with you, but no one knows. So no, I'm not blowing you off," Marcus said. "And, just for the record, Suzanne didn't want to keep this from you, but it isn't her secret to tell. She wanted you to know."

Harold made a rude noise that sounded like a laugh but wasn't. "Then by all means, let's hear it. Does it have anything to do with what Eileen pulled me aside and asked me about regarding the accusation by Rita Mae and her lawyer? Did you do something?"

It was truth time.

He had to glance back, hearing voices from inside. "Let's go talk down here, out of the way."

"You mean so no one can hear."

Marcus didn't bother answering. He started down the stairs, toward Jenny, who was headed across the grass, carrying a square cake pan. "Ryan held up?" he asked.

She wore blue jeans and a jean jacket, her hair hiked up in a ponytail, and he took in the ring on her finger. An engagement? Evidently something else they were going to hear about.

"He should be here soon," she said, then lifted her finger in the air. "We have news." She was all smiles.

He gestured toward it and winked. "Hey, congrats! That's great."

She kept walking into the house, and he could hear the excitement of everyone noticing. Harold, who was standing at the edge of the front lawn, by Suzanne's car, didn't say anything.

"This can't go anywhere," Marcus said.

Harold didn't look away. For a minute, Marcus thought he wouldn't agree. "Did you cover up a crime?" he finally said.

"This was something that happened when I was a kid," Marcus said. "I only just found out about it from Owen. He kept it a secret for years, thinking he was protecting someone..."

Harold furrowed his brow. "Go on, continue. So what does this have to do with what Rita Mae and her lawyer are saying about you? Who was Owen protecting?" He glanced back to the house. "And Suzanne knows?" he added, sounding accusatory.

"Yes, but don't be angry at her. We told her she couldn't tell you, and it just about killed her not to. You should know that Charlotte doesn't know, either. It's just Suzanne, Karen, Ryan, Luke, and me. We only learned of this from Owen, so this isn't some big secret we've been keeping from everyone for a really long time. It's about the night my dad disappeared."

Harold hesitated for a second. Marcus could see that wasn't what he'd expected. It wasn't lost on him that Harold had never agreed not to say anything to anyone.

"There was a fight downstairs while we were asleep," Marcus said. "Owen went down and found our mom upset.

Our dad's office had been wrecked. She handed him a bloody knife wrapped in a cloth and told him to get rid of it. He did, thinking she'd done something. He buried it in the woods, scared, and never told a soul. Apparently, Rita Mae was out there, doing God knows what, and saw him. During the investigation, she said some things to Owen that let him know she'd dug up what he'd buried and kept it all these years. It was then that he came clean to us about what had happened. Would she have been willing to use it against him and me? She threatened as much, holding it over us so we wouldn't look her way in this Jackson thing, but evidently, she had a change of heart, and when Owen paid her a visit, she gave him the knife back. As far as Rita Mae and her lawyer trying to use this now to get her out of this jam… Well, that's everything."

Harold glanced back to the house. The expression on his face was all cop, and Marcus wasn't sure if he'd just screwed himself or Owen, who still wasn't there. "Did your mom kill him?"

It was the question they had all asked. He just shook his head. "We talked to her, and she said no. Something must've happened, because she found his office like that, with a note that said he was gone and not to look for him. No, she didn't do anything. Whose blood it was, I don't know. Our mom said our dad had been having a lot of visitors all of a sudden, and he'd become secretive. Did something happen? Yeah…" He breathed out. "I don't know what, though. Are you going to use this?"

There it was, the million-dollar question of where Harold's loyalties lay.

He gave everything to Marcus. "And have Suzanne kill me? No, I love that woman. But I told her, and I'm telling you, I can't do secrets. What happened to the knife Rita Mae gave Owen?"

Tessa's small compact had pulled up the street, with Owen behind the wheel. His brother had never been this happy.

"Cleaned up, never to be found," Marcus said. "I don't know. I don't want to know."

"Then I guess we have nothing to worry about." Harold gestured with his head to the house just as Owen stepped out of his girlfriend's car. Tessa was laughing. He slung his arm around her shoulder.

"What are you two doing out here?" Owen said.

Marcus felt as if he'd betrayed him, and he dragged his gaze back over to Harold. "Just some work stuff, finishing up," he said, then watched as his brother and Tessa strode into his house. He took in Harold, who was trying to wrap his head around what he'd said.

"A word of advice, Marcus," Harold started when he said nothing. "If I'm wondering what's going on, knowing you and your siblings have a secret, I guarantee you I'm not the only one in this family doing so."

Marcus shook his head. "No one else can know, Harold. This is the kind of thing that could blow up in everyone's face. My mom and Owen would be the ones with their heads on the chopping block," he stressed, hoping he understood.

"You forget about yourself, Marcus."

Maybe it was his expression that had Harold saying, "You're the one who will get burned, being sheriff, coming up on election. If there's any hint of you covering up a crime, hiding a crime like this that's tied to your family, it will be you who's hung out to dry. Not only will you lose your badge, and the job of sheriff, but this could destroy everything you've worked for, and your family."

There it was, that stress of knowing something was hiding, waiting to bite him in the ass. Maybe that was why he felt that uncomfortable tension in his chest again, because he'd just given Harold the one thing he could use against him. Harold reached over and slapped his shoulder.

"Yeah, like Eva," Marcus said. "We could lose her." He took in his house and the man before him, whom he'd known for a long time.

"You're not going to lose her," Harold said. "You think I would do that to you? I've got your back. Stop worrying, but I'm going to say something, only because I'm looking from the outside in. You're a sheriff and a damn good cop, but if this were anyone else, not your mom, who told you that story, would you believe her?"

"Are you calling my mom a liar?" he snapped.

Harold said nothing for a minute and glanced back to the house. "Didn't say that, but, Marcus, you're a good cop. This is too close to home, but I'm telling you, if anyone else tried to tell you that story, you'd be asking the same questions I am. There's something here that doesn't jive. A note, a bloody knife, and no body? Because that's what you're saying."

He looked at the door to the house. He could hear everyone inside. He understood, but at the same time, this was his mom, who'd been there for all of them. "She's my mom, Harold. You know what? You're right, but I'm asking you to leave it alone."

Ryan had pulled in across the street and was getting out of his park ranger's pickup. Marcus turned back to Harold, who had a way about him that could get under a man's skin. It made him a damn good cop.

"I'm just saying, Marcus, if I'm asking these questions, you can be sure I'm not the only one. I'll see you inside." Then he started back to the house.

Marcus took in Ryan, who was crossing the street over to him.

"What was that about?" Ryan asked.

"Just told Harold," he said. "Seems everything is coming to a head."

Ryan said nothing for a second. "Do you think he'll say something?"

He considered it for only a second. "No, no, he won't. But I don't think Mom's telling us everything."

Ryan squinted in the sun and then shook his head. "Yeah, well, I kind of figured that one out." He took a step toward the house. "Got some news to share, too."

"Yeah, about the ring on the finger of the girl you've been living with?" He took in the hint of a teasing smile on Ryan's face.

"She finally said yes," Ryan said as he started up the steps, then strode through.

But Marcus hung back. There was just something in the breeze, in the air, in that moment. He still couldn't shake the feeling that he had left something unsettled, something that could change everything for his family.

Chapter Five

Marcus took in the wire and concrete, thinking of the prison life Reine was stuck in. Nothing about any of this was sitting right with him.

The private for-profit system seemed to be taking over. The corporation that owned this prison owned too many in the country, from juvenile to adult facilities that paid a huge chunk of profit back to the state. He'd never considered it before, but it seemed that tossing people away was big business, and Reine was stuck right in the middle of it.

The system was known for abuse, understaffing, and so much violence. How could anyone locked up come out of there ready to step into society and walk the right road?

He stepped out of the cruiser, taking in the parking lot, only half full. He hadn't told Charlotte he was going to see Reine. He knew she wanted to be there, but then, so did Eva, and the kind of talk he wanted to have with Reine was one on one.

He didn't even know if Reine would see him. He had sent off a quick text to Karen to tell her he was there at the prison, hoping she'd pull whatever strings he couldn't. He stepped inside the building and took in the window and the guard behind it.

"I'm here to see one of your prisoners, Reine Colbert," he said, then showed his sheriff's badge. The man behind the glass slid a clipboard his way. Marcus was well aware he had implied that the visit concerned some type of police business.

"Sign here, Sheriff. You'll have to leave your gun and belt."

He hadn't expected it to be this easy. The man was letting him walk right in, and he hadn't even checked to see whether he was on the list of people Reine wouldn't see. Maybe he was new or didn't care.

"I'll let the guards know," the man continued. Then he heard the click, the buzz of the locks, and the door opened, leading further into the prison, a place he was all too familiar with. He was escorted to a tiny room where he knew lawyers would wait for their clients.

There was no window, just a steel table and chairs. He considered, just for a second, the possibility of losing a little girl he loved more than his next breath. Everything about the shitstorm he could feel himself drowning in seemed to converge in that moment.

He heard the door and turned, taking in Reine, who was led in by one of the guards. Her jumpsuit was baggy, her hair was cut short, and he didn't miss the tattoo on her arm. He wondered whether she'd turn and walk out of there, tell the guard she wouldn't see him.

"Reine, I need to talk with you about Eva," he said before she could say a word—and there it was, a mother's love.

Thankfully, the guard left, and the door was pulled closed. Reine stood for a moment, her eyes filled with so much emotion. Everything about her made Marcus's feeling of unease, which had been building, reach a peak.

"How did you get in here?" she said. "I've specifically asked for you not to be allowed."

So she had been trying to push him away.

"Apparently, it's not that hard to get in when you want to. I need to talk to you about Eva."

"How is she?"

He took a step closer and gestured to a chair at the table, but she only shook her head. Yeah, there was a problem.

"She's happy, she's loved, she keeps asking to see you. You're still her mother, Reine. But I hope you know Charlotte and I love that little girl. She's part of our family."

She didn't nod. "I am her mother, and I believed you would keep her safe."

"She is safe," he said. "Bad things happen, and you know that, but I won't let anything happen to her."

"Was there not a gun to her head? Did a man in your house try to hurt my daughter? I had to hear from one of the guards about what happened..."

So there it was.

"You refused to see me, Reine—and it wasn't quite that way. Yes, there are bad people out there, and I won't lie to you. There was a break-in. She was there with my mother. I got her out. She's okay; I'm making sure of it. So is that why the adoption seems to have come to a standstill? The social worker is stalling, and now I'm hearing that your dad wants to see her. Is this what you want?"

The way she looked at him, so intently, he could feel the anger simmering. "You say she's okay? I want my father to see her, someone I know will tell me the truth. I want to make sure she's okay. I need to know that I made the right choice. I trusted you, Marcus, you and Charlotte, but it seems as of late that trusting the wrong person has left me here, in a life without my daughter."

He could see it in her eyes, her expression, her doubt as to whether Eva should even stay with them, but he wondered if that had more to do with what she was trying to survive in prison. He pulled his arms across his chest and took a step closer to her.

"We love that little girl," he said. "She's part of our family, Reine. You're the one who wanted us to adopt her. She knows we're trying, and you should know that because of these sudden delays, she was asking my niece if we'd changed our minds because she's too much trouble. That's what she thought because of these sudden problems that keep cropping up. I tried to explain to her that this happens, but not to worry, because we are adopting her. It's just taking longer than we expected. Are you going to make a liar out of me?

"You know, when I heard from Alison what Eva feared, I pulled her aside and told her that Charlotte and I will never change our minds, that we'll do whatever it takes to make sure the adoption goes through, because she's our little girl, and we love her. I love her. Charlotte loves her. Don't play with her heart or ours. I'm begging you, Reine. You want your dad to see her, I have no problem with that. I told you so before. But if this is some game you're playing and you want to take her away from us, don't do it."

He didn't know how he would get through to her. She looked away, and he guessed that the one thing he didn't want to be true was.

"Reine, come on," he said. "Be honest, here. This is the only way this works. Are you trying to take Eva away from us? Have you changed your mind now about us adopting her? Please, what's changed for you? I need to know."

She stepped away, and he could see her considering. "I told my father what I heard about the danger she was in, the gunman. He wants to take Eva. She's his granddaughter."

His heart squeezed. "She doesn't know him, Reine—and where was he when you were in trouble, living on the streets?" He knew he was being an asshole, desperate, but he couldn't lose Eva. This would kill Charlotte.

"You already know the answer, Marcus. I never called him because he wasn't in our life..."

"You mean you cut him off, or rather, he cut you off, because you married a man he didn't want for you. You want to give that same fate to Eva?"

She shut her eyes. He could see he'd hit a nerve. "Look, my dad is trying to get me out of here. Don't go there, Marcus. I believed I didn't have a choice. Being in here isn't easy. I never expected the choices I'd have to make in here just to survive."

He let his gaze drop to the prison tattoo, and she crossed her arms. "I know, Reine. If I could make it easier or change things, I would. But I don't have any authority here." For just a moment, he wasn't sure she would believe him. "You asked us to take Eva, and we did. We love her, and she loves you. She still asks to see you. I'm having trouble, Reine. I need you to help me out. How do you think Eva will feel if she's taken away from us now and goes to live with your father, someone she doesn't know? I'll tell you how she'll feel: She'll be angry and hurt, ripped away from us, from her family. We love her. Please don't do this. She has aunts and uncles, a grandmother, a cousin. She's never alone."

"Look, you think I want to hurt my daughter?" she snapped and jammed her hands through her short dark hair. "I want Eva safe, and yes, maybe my dad pointed out to me how hasty I was in telling you to adopt her, in giving her away. Then, hearing from that guard about how she was almost killed... I can live with a lot of things, but I can't live without my daughter. If something happened to her..." She shook her head. She didn't have to say the words. She wouldn't want to go on living.

"How can I reassure you, Reine? I don't want to lose her. Charlotte is pregnant. We're having a baby, a brother or sister for Eva."

"I want my dad to see her," she said. "I need to be reassured that I'm making the right decision."

He knew this was coming down to a man he didn't know anything about. "And then you'll let us adopt her? I need to know, Reine." He knew he couldn't push. Could he win the fight in court? It was a crapshoot, the kind of gamble he couldn't take, not with Eva.

"If my dad is convinced this is best for Eva, that she's happy and that I made the right choice for her, then yes." She stood right in front of him and looked up, and he took in her sadness, the changes in her, and what it was doing to her, being locked away like this.

"Will you let us bring her to see you?"

She considered it for a second. He could see how much she wanted to see her, but she shook her head. "No, I don't want her here. You appease my father, and he gives the green light that she's loved, that's she's happy, that you're giving her everything I can't. Then I'll sign off on all of this, on the adoption."

This was just one more thing that wasn't going the way he'd planned, and it was the one thing he didn't want to tell Charlotte and couldn't tell Eva. He just hoped Mr. MacDonald was, in fact, a man who could be reasoned with.

Chapter Six

He watched as Charlotte set out a tray of veggies on the table in the living room. She wore a white silky blouse and dark blue capris, as well as makeup, which she never wore, and earrings. It all had her looking especially nice.

He could hear his sisters and mom in the kitchen with Eva. He'd basically handed everything at the station over to Harold to deal with: the PJ thing, the issue with which kids had walked and which had gotten screwed. Then there was Rita Mae and her lawyer, who were making the kind of noise that could cast a shadow of doubt onto Marcus and his fitness as an adoptive parent. It could sink everything for his family, just one more scandal that would be the nail in his coffin and end with them losing Eva.

"You know he's just coming to meet Eva," he said. "It's going to be okay. He just has to be convinced we're good people. He just wants to see who we are, meet us, and make sure that..." He looked up and over his wife, knowing his family was keeping Eva distracted in the kitchen.

"He's coming to judge us, Marcus," Charlotte said.

"You know that, and I know that. He's going to pick apart everything, and who knows? He may be coming with his mind already made up."

The screen door squeaked, and he took in Harold as he stepped inside. Right, the whole family was coming over to make a unified front and show Duncan MacDonald that he was walking into the lion's den, and he'd have to go through all of them to get Eva.

"Marcus, you got a second?" Harold said.

He slid his hand over Charlotte's bare arm and down, feeling the tightness in his chest that never seemed to go away. "Yeah," he said, then took in Charlotte, who was so tense. She didn't have a clue about the family secret that Harold now knew. It was something she should know, but at the same time, there were just some things he thought it best she didn't.

"Try to relax, okay?" he said to her, then started over to Harold, who pushed open the door for them to go outside, down the steps.

Marcus took in the cloudy day. He had chosen to dress down, casually, instead of making a point of his role as sheriff. He just had a feeling that the man coming to see him, Reine's father, wouldn't be impressed by that, though he couldn't have explained why.

"Thought you'd want to know that the sentencing for the other kids is tomorrow," Harold said. "The DA is now handling it personally after my conversation with Eileen. You should know I've seen this before, judges taking kickbacks from prisons so they get their numbers, and it always comes down to those who can't fight the system because they lack a good pit-bull of a lawyer. I guarantee you this judge is doing exactly that."

Marcus stared at his deputy. This was just one more

thing he didn't want piled onto his plate. So now there were dirty judges to add to the mix. "This isn't about Jackson Moore anymore," he started.

Harold was already shaking his head. "Was it ever, really? No, sometimes justice works, and sometimes something like this happens. Belinda Lee got screwed big time, while Hunter received a slap on the wrist, and the difference is that the Lees don't have what the Rowses do. Rita Mae got probation, and of the remaining kids, two were going to walk with nothing because they were basically in the wrong place at the wrong time, according to Judge Root. The remaining ones were going to get a mix of community service and five years, depending on whatever kickback the judge was getting.

"I showed up with Eileen in Tibo Lewis's office. I didn't want to make waves, but I said that I wouldn't stand for what was happening, that the sheriff's office would open up an investigation into Judge Root, and we would follow any money trail from the prison to him. I said we'd take it to the Feds, wherever we needed to. You know what Tibo said?"

It took him a second to realize what Harold was doing. "You'd better tell me, considering you making threats like this could have them setting a target on you. Tibo has Judge Root's back. Your job could suddenly disappear. I can't believe you did that."

"Are you saying you wouldn't have done the same thing?" Harold said, and for a second, Marcus could breathe a little easier.

"If I didn't have this Eva thing hanging over my head right now, yeah, I would be doing the same or worse. So what did he say?"

Harold was a solid man, shorter than Marcus, but there was something about him. He could lead where Marcus couldn't. "He didn't like me pointing out that we'd take it to the Feds and start our own investigation. I couldn't believe it when he asked what we wanted. I think Eileen was ready to put his head on a spike, so to speak, because she's the one who said the judge had better reverse every one of his decisions. Having kids locked up was never the deal. Every one of them is to have probation and community service. But this was a felony, and as far as Rita Mae and Hunter, they're to get time. They aren't walking."

This was the kind of agreement that was supposed to happen, Marcus thought. "And...?" He took in a maroon Escalade coming closer, not a vehicle he recognized, but he saw it slowing down.

"He's going to get back to you after he talks with the judge."

The Escalade pulled in front of his house behind Karen's BMW, and Harold too turned to take in the driver behind the wheel. A man, older, of medium build but tall, stepped out and started walking around the front. He wore blue jeans, and his gray hair was neatly trimmed.

"Hello, I'm looking for the O'Connells," he said. This had to be Duncan, Reine's father. He wondered if there was a resemblance there. In the face, maybe.

"I'm Marcus O'Connell," he replied. "You must be Duncan MacDonald, Reine's father." He walked over to the man, and Harold stayed right where he was. Marcus held out his hand, and Duncan seemed to hesitate just a second before shaking it.

"Thanks for agreeing to this," Duncan said.

Marcus was about to remind the man that he'd had his back to the wall, but he didn't. He gestured to Harold. "This is Harold Waters, one of my deputies and my sister's partner."

The man shook Harold's hand, too, and then looked up at the house. Something about this moment felt like D-Day. "So you're a sheriff, I understand—the one who arrested my daughter."

He could feel the judgement, but that wasn't what had happened. "No," he said. "If I'd had my way, Reine wouldn't have been locked up. She was in a bad situation, but I think you know that already. Come on in. You can meet Eva and Charlotte, my wife, and the rest of my family. But just to be clear, Duncan, we love that little girl in there. She's part of our family."

The way the man looked at him, he didn't have a clue what he was thinking. Marcus led him into the house, where he could see the ladies in the kitchen, laughing.

"Hey, everyone," he said. "This is Duncan MacDonald. Duncan, this is my mother, Iris, my sister Karen, my sister Suzanne, Jenny, who is my brother's fiancée, and Alison, my niece."

He thought he heard more voices outside. Ryan was yet to arrive, and Luke, he knew, was still off somewhere, though he didn't have a clue where. They were still missing Owen and Tessa, too.

Duncan was shaking his mom's hand, and he took in Charlotte, who was standing just off to the side, holding Eva in front of her.

"Duncan, this is my wife, Charlotte, and Eva."

The man stepped over, taking in Charlotte. She had both her hands on Eva, who was standing so close to her. He could see how uneasy she was.

"Eva, I'm your grandpa," Duncan said. "I've come a ways to meet you." He actually leaned down, but Eva only hung on to Charlotte, who didn't appear to want to let her go, either. The man looked over to him. "Does she talk?"

What kind of question was that?

"Of course she does," Iris said. "This is my grand-daughter. She's just scared, is all. She doesn't know you, Duncan. Eva, come here." Iris stepped over and ran her hand over Charlotte's shoulder. He could see Eva was close to tears, and Duncan had done nothing to ease her fear.

"Eva, it's okay," Marcus said, squatting down in front of her. "You don't need to be scared. We talked about this." He held out his hands, and she walked over to him.

"But I don't know him," she said. "Is he going to take me away, Marcus? I don't want to leave..."

"Hey, hey, hey, he just wants to meet you," Marcus said. "You're not going anywhere. He's your grandpa, and he wants to get to know you like we know you."

Eva looked up at Duncan and slipped her hand into Marcus's. He wasn't sure what to make of Duncan's expression. He seemed almost human. That was the only thing he could think.

His mom stepped in and said, "You know what, Eva? Let's go hang out in the living room, you and me and your grandpa, and you can tell him all about school and your teacher and maybe show him your room, too..."

Marcus didn't know how his mom had done it, but Eva was holding her hand, and she somehow had Duncan walking with her into the living room. Whatever they were saying, he couldn't make it out. Duncan glanced back to him once before turning the corner.

He took in Charlotte, whose arms were wrapped across her chest. Suzanne, who had been leaning against Harold, strode up behind her and started massaging her shoulders, then kissed her cheek.

"Well, so that's Reine father," Karen said. Marcus realized she was drinking a soda, not something she normally did.

"Where's Jack?" he asked.

She just shrugged. "Oh, he got a call from this deputy who works for you, who told him that some kids were getting screwed over. Me and Jack have stayed as far away from this Jackson Moore thing as we can, but..."

Marcus slid his gaze over to Harold, who only shrugged and said, "I may have forgotten to mention that I called Jack and filled him in."

Karen just shook her head as she rolled her eyes. "He's stepping in to see that the kids who haven't seen any fairness will get some."

Harold gave a subtle smile and shrugged, and Marcus realized his deputy really was going to take care of this situation.

Charlotte stepped over, and his arm slid over her shoulder so she could settle against him as he listened to the back and forth and teasing between Harold, Karen, and Suzanne. Jenny, in the midst of them, had been rather quiet.

"Marcus, Eva is terrified," Charlotte said as she settled her hand over his chest.

"We're here to make sure she's not. It'll be fine."

Charlotte merely sighed. "You have no idea how I hate this feeling of helplessness. I mean, what if he decides we're not good enough, that he's going to take Eva from us?" Her voice was low, but he didn't miss her angst.

"Hey, let's not jump to the worst-case scenario."

"Once he meets all of us, gets to know us, how could he not like us?" Suzanne cut in.

"And don't forget Mom in there, working him with Eva," Karen added. "There's no way he's going to say she's better off with him. I mean, what do we know about him other than the fact that he has no other kids? Isn't he remarried or something? I'm sure that's what Reine said."

Marcus realized Owen and Tessa had arrived and were in the living room, as well, talking with Eva and Duncan. Ryan was also now coming through the front door, and Jenny slipped off the stool as Alison made her way into the living room, as well. So much for a quiet introduction.

He heard laughing, which was always a good sign, and then Karen gestured with her head to the living room and started walking, followed by Harold and Suzanne. That left him alone in the kitchen with Charlotte.

"You know I'm still angry with you for going to see Reine without me yesterday," she said.

"I know, but I wasn't sure I'd get in. I'm glad I didn't take you, because if you'd been there, I wouldn't have gotten in. She still doesn't want to see us."

Charlotte only nodded. "So how is she doing, really?" Of course, Charlotte knew the system and that it was only getting worse for Reine in there.

"She's fitting in a little too well, making the kinds of choices she needs to survive in there. She has a prison tattoo, and I don't know what else. She's in a gang, maybe. Who knows?"

Charlotte didn't say anything as she stepped out of his arms and stood in front of him. "So she's basically coming out more broken than she went in."

He blew out a breath. "She's angry and has every right to be. She got screwed. She's lost her daughter. I just hope she understands we're not the enemy here, and I hope her dad is going to do the right thing."

Charlotte slid her hand over his arm, letting it slide down and linking her fingers with his. "Well, let's not stand here. It seems your family has invaded his visit and is going to force him to get to know them, so we may as well join them and let him see who we are." She took a step, still holding his hand.

"Fine, so you think jamming our family down his throat is a good idea?" he said as he started walking with her, hearing laughter and talking and teasing and Eva and Alison's back and forth.

"Well, you know what? It's kind of what you all did with all of us, right? Harold, Jack, Tessa, Jenny... You O'Connells are a strange bunch, all about family, knowing each other's secrets."

For a second, when she said that and looked at him, he thought she knew something. Then she stepped in closer and slid her hands over his chest so he could lean down and kiss her.

"Don't look so worried," she said. "You think I don't know you have secrets with your siblings? We all do, but I guess I figured if you wanted me to know, you'd tell me." She pulled away and stepped back, then started into the living room, and all he could think was how much he loved this woman. There was no way in hell he was letting Duncan MacDonald take Eva from them.

He considered the situation for a second before stepping into the living room, seeing his mother and Duncan off to the side. Whatever she was saying to him had him giving her all his attention, one on one. It took him only a second to realize that his mom was already working on him.

Chapter Seven

There was a tap on Marcus's open office door, and he looked up to see Harold. He didn't know what to make of the expression on his deputy's face as he stepped into his office and closed the door.

"Do I want to hear this?" he said.

Harold took another second, seeming to consider his answer. Just the night before, he'd stood shoulder to shoulder with Owen, Ryan, Karen, and Suzanne beside him, letting them know he knew about the knife and what had happened. Marcus wasn't sure Owen agreed with what he'd done, considering he'd yet to say anything to him.

Harold pushed away from the door and started over to Marcus, who closed up another burglary file he had no leads on, this time for a bunch of missing scrap metal.

"Was just at the courthouse and wanted to let you know that Tibo pulled me aside, said the judge had a change of heart and reversed the sentences for the kids. He threw the book at the ones he'd let walk before. They're all back home now. He also agreed to recuse himself, but don't get too excited, as it seems Judge Thompson will be stepping in now. Tibo made it clear that any trail I'm looking for, I won't find it, and there's nothing wrong with campaign donations from a corporation. It's just because the judge didn't want to be accused of impropriety that he's agreeing to step down."

Marcus leaned back in his chair, which squeaked. "You mean it was that easy?"

An odd smile touched Harold's lips, and he shook his head as he stepped up to the desk and looked down at Marcus. "Oh, no, I'd say it's more that whatever Jack said yesterday had the judge rethinking the wisdom of what he was doing. He's cleaned up the trail so nothing can be linked to him. The judge is smart, and the DA... Well, Tibo—"

"Tibo won't derail the gravy train, because taking on a sitting judge, any judge, would be career suicide."

"Yeah, but don't you think Tibo knew what the judge was doing?" Harold was a smart man, and Marcus knew he'd seen his share of things in the different states and cities he'd worked in.

"Of course. Tibo isn't a stupid man. Of course he knew, but it comes down to that age-old bullshit of looking the other way. So Judge Thompson, huh?" Marcus said. "And Eileen, is she still sidelined or are the original deals back on the table now for everyone involved?"

"Probation for all the kids is what's on the table," Harold said, "but for Hunter and Rita Mae, it's jail time Eileen's aiming for. Whether she'll get it, we'll see. Tibo has taken a special interest and wants this shut down quickly. Apparently, he had a word with Rita Mae and her lawyer. Not sure what he said, but whatever it was, they're no longer saying anything about you or Owen."

It took him another second to understand what Harold

was saying. "So Tibo shut it down, as in, he's going to think I owe him one?" Just saying it left him with a sick feeling in his stomach.

Harold shook his head and glanced away before giving him everything. "Yeah, well, you'll know when he comes calling." He settled his hands on his waist, over his duty belt, and then added, "And PJ's here, outside, waiting to talk to you."

Marcus was on his feet and started around the desk. "You couldn't have started with that?" he said. He wasn't sure if there was amusement in Harold's expression as he pulled open the door, taking in PJ, bearded, in faded jeans and a worn T-shirt, talking with Charlotte. "PJ, come on in," he called.

Whatever Charlotte had been saying to him, PJ seemed rather calm. She reached over and touched his arm with such compassion. PJ started Marcus's way, his heavy boots digging in with each step. He had lines etched around his eyes, and Marcus wondered how much sleep the man was getting. Charlotte reached out to him, her expression filled with sympathy, as PJ walked into his office, and he followed him and closed the door.

"You know Harold, my deputy," Marcus said, gesturing to Harold, who stood by the door. He wondered what PJ was after, what he needed or wanted other than getting justice for his son, who had been the victim in all this. "What brings you down here, PJ?"

"Wanted to let you know that I heard what happened, with that judge stepping down."

"What he did wasn't okay," Marcus said. "But this isn't done, PJ. A new judge is taking over. The kids are going to be held accountable. Everyone is."

PJ dragged his gaze over to Harold and then back to

him. "And the pills? Told you I wasn't going to let it go. I want to know whose they were. I have a right to know."

What the hell was he supposed to say? PJ didn't have that right, yet he should.

"The opiates were from a prescription given to Angela Rowse, Hunter's mother," Marcus said. "I'm not sure how this will help, knowing, but you're right. You do have a right to know. We also think the judge was taking kickbacks from the private prisons for every kid he sent there. My deputy figured it out, talked with the DA. No one's getting an unfair shake here, and no one's walking scot free, not without a fight." He wasn't sure what to make of the way PJ was watching him.

"This is about justice for Jackson," he continued. "He's going to get it; you have my word. At the same time, I need to know that you're not going to try to get retribution from the Rowses. Hunter is going to be held accountable. It was a stupid thing those kids did. You know it, and I know it—but it's not that different from when we went to school."

PJ understood what he was talking about, Marcus knew, considering the path they had both walked. "I'm not looking for trouble, Marcus, but I had a right to know everything. Just saying, as long as justice is served, then you have no quarrel with me." Then he did something unexpected: He held out his hand to him.

Marcus hesitated for only a second before shaking it.

"Thank you, Marcus, for keeping your word," PJ said. Then he started past him to the door, but before he opened it, he glanced back. "And just so you know, since you did keep your word, you have my gratitude. Give my best to your family."

Then he was gone, and for a minute, all Marcus could

do was stare at the open door. He turned to Harold and gestured with his thumb. "Did that just happen?"

Harold shook his head. "Yeah, well, I'd take that as a win. I'd rather have PJ on our side than not…"

He thought he heard Karen out in the office, saying something to PJ and Charlotte. He stepped out with Harold just as PJ left. Karen was in heels and a long skirt, her hair hanging loose and a big smile on her face.

"Hey, just the person I wanted to see!" she said. "You and Charlotte. I've got good news, and I wanted to do this in person." She set her bag on Charlotte's desk and pulled out a piece of paper, then handed it to her.

"What is that?" Marcus said. The tightness in his chest had returned.

"It's Reine's signature on the adoption form," Karen said. "Seems Duncan was so impressed with us and our family, and with how happy Eva is and how much we love her, that he spoke with Reine and told her to sign it."

Marcus was standing right beside Charlotte now, and he took in the paper for the adoption. For a second, he couldn't speak, maybe from relief at the absence of the weight that had been on his shoulders for so long.

"It's real? This is real?" Charlotte said, then looked up at him, her eyes misty.

"So real that it's just a formality now," Karen said. "We'll go before the judge, and I'll have a date set today. Then Eva will be Eva O'Connell, the newest member of our family. Oh, and, by the way, it seems Mom has invited Duncan for the celebration. She said something about how he was still in town, alone. His second marriage ended."

He wasn't sure he'd heard right. Harold gave him a thumbs-up before walking over to his desk and answering the ringing phone.

"Mom's invited Duncan?" Marcus said. "Sounds like she's gotten to know him."

Charlotte slid her arm around his waist. "I'm just happy he signed it. Let him come. But you know what this means?"

Marcus nodded. "Yeah, it means this is almost over. Eva will be ours."

"She's already ours—all of ours," Karen added, then inclined her head and started over to Harold, who'd hung up the phone.

Marcus turned to Charlotte, resting his hand on her shoulder. "You know what? How about you and I take the rest of the day off?"

Charlotte made a face and slid her hands over his chest. "And what would the sheriff say to that?" she said with a lot of sass and teasing, without the stress she'd carried for so long, worrying about losing Eva.

"Well, I happen to have an in with him," Marcus said. He winked, then leaned and kissed her, letting it linger a second. When he pulled back and took in her face and the love she had for him, he knew there might come a time when he had no choice but to tell her the secrets he had been keeping.

"What's wrong?" She slid her hand over his face, and he pressed a kiss to her palm and shook his head.

"It's all good. Let's go and tell Eva. You know I love you, right?"

She tilted her head, and her eyes softened. "I know you do. So let's go before the phone starts ringing or the sheriff comes to his senses and changes his mind," Charlotte said, reaching for her purse and sliding her hand in his.

He opened the door, glancing over to Harold, who was

talking with his sister. He knew that his deputy would have his back.

His family was together, and disaster had been averted, but what was next for the O'Connells? Whatever it was, as he followed his wife out the door of the station and took in the town where he'd grown up, he still couldn't shake the feeling that something else was brewing.

Turn the page for a sneak peek of
*THE FAMILY SECRET the next book in THE
O'CONNELLS*
Available in print, eBook & audio

THE FAMILY SECRET

Raymond O'Connell was the love of Iris's life— from the day she met him, to the day a year later when she married him, to the tragic night before she never saw him again.

Some would say they had the perfect all-American life. Now, eighteen years later, questions arise about the night her husband disappeared, leaving a bloody knife and a letter addressed to her, in which he said goodbye and told her not to look for him, with not even a second thought for her and their six children.

The scandal when Raymond left rocked the community, fueling widespread rumors, from him running away with his mistress to him being dead. But through it all, Iris kept her head down, keeping the secret of what really happened. Although her children often wondered, and her eldest thought he was protecting her from something heinous when she asked him to get rid of the knife, what they didn't know was that their father wasn't who they thought he was. Making sure his secret didn't come out was the only way to keep her family together.

Now, Iris can no longer keep her life with Raymond O'Connell buried, because her adult children are asking questions. The only thing she can think to do to protect herself and them is to enlist the help of a lawyer, her daughter's husband, fearing that once the truth starts to surface, it could change everything about their lives.

The secret of their father, which Iris has hidden for so long now, has the potential to destroy everything the O'Connells have built for themselves, and once the truth of who Raymond O'Connell really was comes out, it will put a target on all of them, and their lives in peaceful Livingston, Montana, will never be the same.

The Family Secret, Chapter 1

AT ONE TIME, IF ANYONE HAD TRIED TO TELL IRIS SHE would end up with the stable life she had now, she'd have told them they were crazy. For so many years, she'd kept her head down, putting everything on hold for her children and pushing away that hurt, that ache, that pain that had shredded her heart, having to climb out of the dark pit that wanted to drag her down.

Now, as she pulled in a breath, she had to remind herself that she no longer felt that guttural ache that had stolen her peace of mind and distracted her from all those small things that should've put a smile on her face in her children's early years. She'd forgotten exactly when it had happened, when that wretched, visceral ache, which she'd screamed into a pillow to ease, had just left.

Her six children, whom she couldn't imagine a life without, were all grown now, and she still centered every-thing around them. Her life was theirs. At the same time, there were days she wondered whether she had perma-nently scarred them, whether she could've done better.

She took in the concrete buildings, the bustling streets,

the restaurants and bars and stores, and the scent of the autumn day on the breeze. These people made Livingston her home. It was a part of who she was, though there were times she had to tell herself she wasn't a fraud.

The light of day seemed so different from the shadows of night. The darkness still called to her when she was alone, looking out into the yard. She wondered what was hiding there, what was waiting to tear down the façade she'd built and take away everything that put a smile on her face, all the reasons she could now hold her head high. It was just a feeling she couldn't shake, one that had suddenly reemerged the moment her children learned of the night she wished she could forget.

She lifted her hand in a wave at a couple she knew, then another neighbor, people she knew well had gossiped behind her back at one time after she went from being a married woman to a single mother, struggling alone with six kids. It had cut her to the quick. Yes, Raymond O'Connell had been there one day and gone the next, and the rumors about why had left her feeling more alone than anything.

Of course it still smarted, if she really thought about it now. How did one go about shaking off all those hurtful rumors? People had trashed her character, saying she wasn't good enough, that she must've done something to deserve such a fate, that she was screwing up big-time when it came to her kids, all because the O'Connells no longer fit the all-American mold of how a family was supposed to be.

She clutched her bargain-bin purse, wearing a plain white T-shirt and loose red cardigan over slimming blue jeans. She didn't have to look in a mirror to know that while she was just Mom around her grown children, any man out there would've given her a second look. It was just who she was. Even though time hadn't been her friend, her lack of money while the kids were young had kept her from eating her way into a pity party. She was grateful for that, at least, considering being slim and attractive had been the furthest thing from her mind for too many years.

She took in the nightclub in front of her, where staff were serving the lunch crowd, then turned to the glass industrial door with the words "Karen O'Connell & Jack Curtis, Lawyers" etched in black. An office over a nightclub. She couldn't help the smile that tugged at her lips.

She was so proud of her daughter Karen, a lawyer, and Karen's husband, Jack, who had a charm and charisma about him that reminded her so much of her own husband. Maybe that was why she watched him from a distance, wondering when he'd turn into someone else. There was something about him that told her he was holding on to the kind of secrets he would never share with another person. How did she know? It was just one of those feelings she got about people she spent time with.

She knew there was so much more to his life and his secrets than she would ever know, but she also knew he'd do anything for her daughter.

Iris forced herself to touch the steel handle and pull open the door, feeling it scrape against the metal lip on the ground. She started up the steps, her shoes squeaking to announce her arrival. Her palms sweated, and her heart kicked up with each step. She made herself pull in a breath.

She could hear talking, a man's voice—Jack, she thought —as she stepped up on the landing, her hand on the rail, taking in the narrow hall and the open office door. The walls were dingy, nicked, and needed a fresh coat of paint.

She stepped into the reception area, seeing the door to Karen's office closed. Jack was sitting at the receptionist's desk, a position they still hadn't filled. He lifted his hand in a wave to her, the phone to his ear, his blue eyes mysterious and his dark hair neatly groomed. He already had a five o'clock shadow, and it was barely noon. He hung up the phone and stood.

"Iris, I didn't know you were coming by," he said, gesturing toward her and walking around the desk. "Karen is actually in court right now."

She shook her head, taking in his blue striped dress shirt and dark pants. He was attractive, and she wondered, looking at him now, what it was about him that gave her that sense of familiarity, reminding her of a man she'd once thought of dozens of times a day—a man who, thankfully, had now become just a passing thought.

"That's fine," Iris said. "I actually stopped by to see you. Do you have a minute?"

She wasn't sure what he was thinking. He hesitated, and a soft smile touched his lips as he leaned against the desk and crossed his arms, giving her everything with just a look. She glanced over her shoulder to the open door and then back to him.

"You know what?" he said. "Let's go talk in the office. Seems my wife and I can't decide on a new place. She likes this dump, and we end up having to share an office, or one of us works out in reception..." He opened the office door and walked in, then stepped aside so he could close it behind her.

He had evidently picked up on her unease and her need for privacy, even though she didn't have a clue what she was going to say. He gestured to the chairs in front of the desk, and she squeezed her purse over her shoulder.

"Please, Iris, have a seat," he said. "So you wanted to talk to me?"

She walked over to the chair and sat down, and she

expected him to sit behind the desk across from her, but instead he sat beside her. Something in his blue eyes was so intense. He didn't look away, didn't pull away. He seemed amused, curious, but she wondered how curious he'd be when he learned the truth of what she'd done and who she really was.

There it was, silence, because she'd missed her cue to speak.

She slid her purse strap off her shoulder and took her time setting it on the floor. When she looked up, he was still waiting patiently.

"Is everything all right, Iris?" he said, then glanced to the door and back to her. He leaned forward, his forearms resting on his knees, and she took in the scar along the side of his face, tiny, just barely there. He started to laugh and rubbed the back of his head. "Are you upset with me or something?"

She gestured toward him. "No, no, nothing like that. I just need a second to find the words or rip the bandage off, so to speak. You know, Karen doesn't know I've come here, and neither do my other children..." She hesitated.

Jack glanced to the door again and sat up straighter, an odd smile touching his lips. "Okay. You do know that whatever you say to me, I won't share it. It stays between us."

She reached for her purse and unzipped it, then opened up her wallet, seeing the bills inside. She pulled out a dollar bill and rested it on the desk, one hand pressed over it as she clutched her wallet in the other.

He inhaled and stared at her hand. Evidently, he had figured out this was something more than a friendly visit.

"I want to hire you as my lawyer, Jack," she said, then pushed the bill closer to him.

His expression had suddenly turned serious as he

dragged his gaze over to her. His blue eyes were so different from the O'Connell blue. He hesitated, and all she did was lower her gaze to the money on the desk beside him, forcing a swallow past the lump in her throat and fighting the instinctual tremble in her hand.

"Is it true that as my lawyer, you can't share anything?" she said, though she knew it was, considering she'd listened to everything Karen had shared with her during her studies to become a lawyer—every law, all the rights, everything that could be used against someone.

Jack pulled in a breath, hesitating only a second before he settled his hand over the bill and held it up. "Okay, so this is a retainer?" He didn't laugh. He could obviously see that she had no intention of saying a word until he said what she needed to hear.

"Yes, consider me your lawyer," he said, then shoved the dollar bill in his pocket. He stood up and walked around the desk, changing from her daughter's husband to a business-man. Maybe he needed to have something between them to ensure a level of professionality.

She did, too, but more for courage, because she couldn't remember feeling the kind of fear she was feeling right now. She wondered whether he could hear her relief as she breathed out.

"So you're looking for a will or something done up?" he said. The way he asked, it sounded as if he couldn't imagine anything else. He actually reached for a legal pad in one of Karen's drawers and rummaged for a pen as Iris silently wished it were that simple.

"I married a man and had six of his children only to learn he wasn't the man I thought he was," she said. "The night he left, I did something."

Jack leaned on the desk, ready to write, and froze, pen

in hand. He slowly dragged his gaze up and over to her, and she had to force herself to continue before the fear that was threatening to choke her took over and shut down her voice. Her throat was thick, and she cleared it.

"I'm afraid that one day very soon, there will be a knock on my door, a reckoning for what I did and what I know. In fact, I can already feel it, something coming, whispering that my time is up."

She'd expected shock, maybe outrage, not the stillness that was staring back at her. He opened his mouth to say something, but instead he simply stood up, walked over to the door, and locked it.

When he turned, she could see he needed a minute to get his head around the bomb she'd just dropped. He started back to the desk, digging into each step, but instead of sitting, he rested his hands on the back of the chair right beside her and leaned down. His gaze was imploring, intense, and she knew she had all his attention.

"Okay, I think you'd better start at the beginning," he said, "and don't leave anything out."

About the Author

"Lorhainne Eckhart is one of my go to authors when I want a guaranteed good book. So many twists and turns, but also so much love and such a strong sense of family."

(Lora W., Reviewer)

New York Times & USA Today bestseller Lorhainne Eckhart writes Raw Relatable Real Romance is best known for her big family romances series, where "Morals and family are running themes. Danger, romance, and a drive to do what is right will see you glued to the page." As one fan calls her, she is the "Queen of the family saga." (aherman) writing "the ups and downs of what goes on within a family but also with some suspense, angst and of course a bit of romance thrown in for good measure." Follow Lorhainne on Bookbub to receive alerts on New Releases and Sales and join her mailing list at LorhainneEckhart.com for her Monday Blog, books news, giveaways and FREE reads. With over 120 books, audiobooks, and multiple series published and available at all retailers now translated into six languages. She is a multiple recipient of the Readers' Favorite Award for Suspense and Romance, and lives in the Pacific Northwest on an island, is the mother of three, her oldest has autism and she is an advocate for never giving up on your dreams.

"Lorhainne Eckhart has this uncanny way of just hitting the spot every time with her books."

(Caroline L., Reviewer)

The O'Connells: _The O'Connells of Livingston, Montana are not your typical family. A riveting collection of stories surrounding the ups and downs of what goes on within a family but also with some suspense, angst and of course a bit of romance thrown in for good measure "I thought I loved the Friessens, but I absolutely adore the O'Connell's. Each and every book has totally different genres of stories but the one thing in common is how she is able to wrap it around the family which is the heart of each story." (C. Logue)_

The Friessens: _An emotional big family romance series, the Friessen family siblings find their relationships tested, lay their hearts on the line, and discover lasting love! "Lorhainne Eckhart is one of my go to authors when I want a guaranteed good book. So many twists and turns, but also so much love and such a strong sense of family." (Lora W., Reviewer)_

The Parker Sisters: *The Parker Sisters are a close-knit family, and like any other family they have their ups and downs. "Eckhart has crafted another intense family drama...The character development is outstanding, and the emotional investment is high..." (Aherman, Reviewer)*

The McCabe Brothers: *Join the five McCabe siblings on their journeys to the dark and dangerous side of love! An intense, exhilarating collection of romantic thrillers you won't want to miss. — "Eckhart has a new series that is definitely worth the read. The queen of the family saga started this series with a spin-off of her wildly successful Friessen series." From a Readers' Favorite award—winning author and "queen of the family saga" (Aherman)*

Lorhainne loves to hear from her readers! You can connect with me at:
www.LorhainneEckhart.com
lorhainneeckhart.le@gmail.com

In the Family
In the Silence
In the Charm
Unexpected Consequences
It Was Always You
The First Time I Saw You
Welcome to My Arms
Welcome to Boston
I'll Always Love You
Ground Rules
A Reason to Breathe
You Are My Everything
Anything For You
The Homecoming
Stay Away From My Daughter
The Bad Boy
A Place of Our Own
The Visitor
All About Devon
Long Past Dawn
How to Heal a Heart
Keep Me In Your Heart

The O'Connells
The Neighbor
The Third Call
The Secret Husband
The Quiet Day
The Commitment
The Missing Father
The Hometown Hero
Justice
The Family Secret

The Fallen O'Connell
The Return of the O'Connells
And The She Was Gone
The Stalker
The O'Connell Family Christmas
The Girl Next Door

The McCabe Brothers
Don't Stop Me (Vic)
Don't Catch Me (Chase)
Don't Run From Me (Aaron)
Don't Hide From Me (Luc)
Don't Leave Me (Claudia)
Out of Time

A Billy Jo McCabe Mystery
Nothing As it Seems
Hiding in Plain Sight
The Cold Case
The Trap
Above the Law

The Wilde Brothers
The One (Joe and Margaret)
The Honeymoon, A Wilde Brothers Short
Friendly Fire (Logan and Julia)
Not Quite Married, A Wilde Brothers Short
A Matter of Trust (Ben and Carrie)
The Reckoning, A Wilde Brothers Christmas
Traded (Jake)
Unforgiven (Samuel)
The Holiday Bride

Married in Montana
His Promise
Love's Promise
A Promise of Forever

The Parker Sisters
Thrill of the Chase
The Dating Game
Play Hard to Get
What We Can't Have
Go Your Own Way
A June Wedding

Kate & Walker
One Night
Edge of Night
Last Night

Walk the Right Road Series
The Choice
Lost and Found
Merkaba
Bounty
Blown Away: The Final Chapter

The Saved Series
Saved
Vanished
Captured

Single Titles
He Came Back

Loving Christine

For my German Readers
Die Außenseiter-Reihe
Der Vergessene Junge
Der Gefallene Held

For my French Readers
L'ENFANT OUBLIÉ